DEAD MALL

Part IV
The Mourning Sun

ALSO BY S.G. TASZ

<u>The Dead Mall Series</u>
An Original Sin
Welcome to Halcyon
Veiled Threats
The Long Moon
A Midwinter Nightmare
The Lost Weekend
Everything Must Go
The January Hours Collection

<u>Other Works</u>
Mr. Lucky

DEAD MALL

THE MOURNING SUN

S.G. Tasz

The Uglycat Press
Las Vegas, NV

This is a work of fiction. Names, characters, places and incidents are either the product of the author's imagination or are used fictitiously. Any resemblance to actual persons, living or dead, business establishments, events, or locales is purely coincidental.

No part of this publication may be reproduced or transmitted in any form, or by any means (electronic, mechanical, photocopying, recording or otherwise), without the prior written permission of the author. Reproduction in whole or part of this publication without express written consent of the author is strictly prohibited.

Copyright © 2021 by S.G. Tasz

Editing services provided by Chimera Editing
www.chimeraediting.com

Cover art by Joseph Reedy.

All rights reserved.

ISBN: 978-1-7340752-8-1

To family near and far, far away.

Chapter One

Grace vaulted down the stairs toward the bunker so fast her boots barely touched the steps. John's words chased her the whole way down.

"Ray's dead."

She'd been home for maybe ten minutes when he'd called. Barely enough time to shove a handful of crackers in her mouth and toss her work clothes in the laundry.

Well, not all her clothes. Her tank top, bra, leggings and underwear had been donated to the incinerator thanks to the infected purple goo-sweat they'd been stewing in for the last four hours. Even if they'd looked at all salvageable, there was no way in hell she'd risk introducing that crap to the city water supply.

Then the phone rang. Not her cell, but the ancient rotary phone stuck to the wall over the narrow peninsula that separated her kitchenette from the living room/bedroom/rest of her tiny bungalow. The jangle of the old-timey bell filled her with dread. Three people in the world had that number, and they only used it when something was really, really wrong.

Which, of course, something was.

Ray's dead.

She landed at the bottom of the stairs with a thud. Her fingers flicked over the keypad without hesitation. She raced past the lockers toward the detention cells, where a drooling Holly pressed her puke-green cheek against the first window. Grace wrinkled her nose at the undead thing stroking the double-thick plastic with her tattered fingertips, her yellowed eyes fluttering in a droopy-lidded half-coma.

At last, she blasted through the door of the med station. John's head shot up from the cot where he was smoothing out a new sheet. The sight of his bloodshot eyes, pasty skin and sloping shoulders hit her like a bucket of ice. Based on his reaction, her own appearance wasn't much better. She'd left in such a hurry she'd barely had time to wrap her uncombed black curls into a handkerchief, and she wore the faded backup coveralls she kept balled up in her closet for emergencies. She hadn't even had time to shower, and her light brown skin looked ashy, even a little purple still, from the previous night's exploits. But it didn't matter. Nothing mattered except being here.

She shambled across the room and collapsed into his arms. "What happened? I thought he had time." Her voice, buried in the shoulder of his cinnamon-scented sweater vest, sounded soft and small, even to her own ears.

"We all did," John murmured. "Massive coronary. There was nothing they could do."

"Did you call Mimi?"

"A few minutes ago. I offered condolences to her and to Lola, who I'm told is on her way back from Honolulu now to help with the arrangements. She said the funeral will likely be next weekend. A small service, just family and a few close friends."

"Good," Grace whispered, unwilling to ask if that included her. Beyond the walls of Edensgate, the three of them appeared to be nothing more than colleagues: she, a mid-level employee; John, her boss; and Ray, the manager that had contracted them to fulfill the mall's security and maintenance needs—until last week, that is, when he'd retired due to his failing health. It was a business relationship, and a past-tense one at that. If anyone knew the real history of their bond, not only would she and John be invited to the funeral, they would be seated in the front row.

Or run out of town on a rail.

She gave John one more light squeeze around the waist, then extracted herself from his arms. "And there's no way to know if this will affect…you know, this place?"

"No." He sighed and rubbed the back of his neck. "We'll have to keep an eye out for anything—"

The insistent buzz at her hip made her cringe. John stared at her pocket like it was full of snakes.

"…strange."

Grace's hand shook as she checked the caller ID. A local number, but no contact name associated with it. *Please,* she prayed as she pressed the green button. *Please be a solicitor. A wrong number. Even—*

"Hello, my name is Polly with the Green Sun Initiative."

"Oh, thank God," Grace exhaled, her arms and legs going liquid with relief.

"Oh my! Well…thank you very much. I'm glad to be speaking with you too. Would you agree to take a quick 10-minute survey about a proposed bill regarding—"

"Grace!"

She nearly sent her phone flying as she whirled around to face the door, and the trembling ball of black and blond streaking toward her.

"Cari?" Grace braced herself for impact, but the younger girl skidded to a halt mere inches from the collision point. "What's wrong?"

"I second that," came a voice from the doorway. Grace looked from Cari as Rex wandered into the room, clad in sweats, a tattered black t-shirt and extremely dingy socks. The white gauze bandages wrapped around both forearms practically glowed against his russet skin, evidence of his own trials from the previous night. "I was about to slay RenoKing78 at MegaBall, so this better be good."

Grace rolled her eyes, made sure the call was disconnected, and turned her attention back to Cari. The girl's delicate body heaved, presumably from exertion, as she struggled to catch her breath. Then her blue eyes turned upward, and Grace saw the real reason for her breathlessness.

Panic.

"I think…I think I may have killed someone," Cari heaved.

Grace's knees buckled. Luckily, John had the presence of mind to grab her by the elbow before she could fully collapse.

"Sorry, I think I misheard you." Rex ambled in to join them, smiling to disguise the tremble in his voice. "From where I was standing it sounded like you said you killed someone."

"Who?" John prompted as Grace composed herself. "Who was it?"

"Nelson Baines. My mom's…um, boyfriend, I guess. He was there when I got home, and he was doing…something, to her. So, I threw an ax at him." She bit her lip as her eyes filled with tears. "I didn't mean to do it. Or…I don't know, maybe I did. It's hard to remember. Everything sort of went black and brown and fuzzy. One second my hand was empty, and then I had the ax and then…it hit him." She swallowed like she was trying not to be sick. "It hit him in the face."

"Damn," Rex muttered, his smile long gone. "Are you sure he's dead?"

"Well…I'm sure he *was* dead. He just didn't…stay that way."

The words lingered in the air like the smell of rotten meat. Rex gaped at Cari as if she'd slapped him across the mouth. Grace could feel her mind trying to untether itself from her reason, and she was tempted to let it happen. She wanted to disappear, to let the panic overtake her.

What made her yank her wits back into her head was the terrified puppy look on Cari's face, her huge eyes darting between John and herself, pleading silently for their help.

She's one of us now. Whatever happens, we can't let her go through this alone.

Grace took a breath, shook John's hand off her, and forced herself onto her own feet.

"Okay," she said with as much surety as she could muster. "Where is Nelson now?"

"My house," Cari said. "I locked him in when I left."

"And your mom?"

"In the car. She was unconscious so I dragged her into the back seat."

"And the car is…?"

"In the parking lot."

Grace frowned. "I thought you couldn't drive."

The left corner of Cari's mouth tugged down, and she stared at her feet. "Um, well…"

"It's okay," John cut in, placing his fingers lightly on Grace's shoulders. "I think we can leave moving violations on the back burner for the time being. Take us to your mom."

Nodding, Cari booked it out of the room with Rex close on her heels.

"After you, Boss." Grace swept her hand in front of John like a footman in front of a king. "Wouldn't want you to cut me off twice in a row."

He rolled his eyes as he jogged passed. "Am I wrong?"

She grunted her acquiescence. Of course, he wasn't wrong. A half-beheaded demon-murderer trapped in a rickety trailer was the definition of bigger fish to fry. But she wasn't in love with the thought of Cari whipping down the pitted desert highway in her mother's junky little coupe either.

They emerged one by one into the pale pink dawn. The smell of frost hung in the air, edged with the foul stench of scorched rubber and gasoline. As they cleared the wide columns of the entrance, they confronted the source of the smell: a rusted red car, its front wheels popped over the curb and its face hugging a lamppost.

"Damn, Mayhem," Rex said, waving the acrid fumes away from his face.

"Told you," Grace mumbled in John's direction. He glared a few half-hearted daggers at her, then approached the crumpled vehicle. Both doors were closed, and the windows were coated with gray condensation so thick it was impossible to see inside.

Grace turned to Cari. "You said Nelson was doing something to her when you walked in?"

"Yeah." Cari nodded, her freckled forehead a patchwork of worry lines. In front of them, John leaned down to try and get a better look through the rear passenger window. "At first, I thought they were just…you know, making out or whatever."

"Ew!" Rex grimaced.

"I know. But then he stopped, and he looked up at me, and--"

A muffled growl rankled the quiet morning, followed by a dull thud as the face of Cari's mother burst into view inches from John's nose. He yelped and sprang backward like a spooked cat.

Grace dashed forward, fists up and ready for blows. Luckily, the window was stronger than the rest of the car, because it hadn't even cracked. Screaming in frustration, Libby Hembert slammed her forehead against the glass again. Still, it held strong as a puddle of thick, black liquid seeped from the torn patch of skin on her forehead. Gnashing teeth squeaked over the glass as gangrenous palms slapped and smeared the fog. Her eyes weren't black, as Grace had expected, but swirling gray and opaque. They reminded her of the thick ominous murk that lingered in the air over a deep canyon, disguising the reality that there was, in fact, no bottom.

From behind her came a soft, fragile whimper. Without turning, Grace slid a foot or so to her right, putting herself between Cari and the growing black blotch on the glass.

"What now?" she whispered at John.

"Same as always." He slid a hardback leather case from his pants pocket. Unzipping it revealed a set of hypodermic needles and a small vial of red liquid. "Sedation, then isolation protocol."

The stoniness of his words chilled her to the core. "That only ends one way."

"We don't have another option." John sucked the red liquid into the needle. "I don't know how, but the Edensgate perimeter has been breached. We have to limit the number of casualties." He slipped the case back in his pocket, held the syringe needle-up, and flicked the chamber. "You go left. I'll be the distraction."

"Fine. But make it quick. The kid's been through enough already." She pivoted in place toward Cari and Rex. "Keys."

Cari fished the ring out of her pocket and tossed them at Grace. Though Cari's eyes never left her toes, Grace had no problem snatching the projectile out of the air. The girl had truly remarkable aim.

Grace dropped into a squat and duck-walked toward the parking lot. When she was sure those hazy eyes had lost track of her, she doubled back, circling the car, and hunched next to the front wheel. Meanwhile John inched closer, hands up, muttering placations in a soothing tone. When he was about three feet away, he stopped. Grace ventured a look upward. Libby's ghoulish face was still suctioned to the window, completely absorbed by John's unwavering stare. She grinned at him and flicked the tip of its blue-gray tongue against the glass like a snake.

Shivering, Grace returned her attention to John. He held up an index finger. Stretching long, she hooked a hand under the cold metal car handle. He held up a second finger, the muscles in his legs and arms tensing ever so slightly. With her other hand, she located the unlock button on the car's key fob.

He held up his third finger.

She pressed the button and yanked the door open. Libby tumbled forward; her huff of surprise was quickly subverted by a spiraling screech as she smashed face-first into the cement.

John descended and plunged the syringe into her neck. She spasmed, emitted one last pitiful croak, then crumbled into a lumpy, sweater-and-jean-skirted heap on the sidewalk.

"Mom!" Grace heard Cari scream. She looked up in time to see Rex grab her by the arm, halting her rush in their direction.

Grace caught his eye and jerked her head toward the door. He winked in solemn understanding, then gently ushered Cari inside.

Satisfied, she turned back to the twisted mass of semi-humanity in front of her. Libby's head lay on her right ear, face turned in Grace's direction. Most of her front teeth were cracked or broken. Black blood flowed from both mouth and nose as well as forehead. But at least those eyes were closed now. She listened for a moment to the wet, ragged breath wheezing from that destroyed mouth.

"Breathing," she muttered. "Like *people* do. That's a good sign, right?"

"I don't know." John rolled the unconscious woman onto her back before gathering her up in his arms. "We don't know what we're dealing with yet, so…maybe. But don't get your hopes up."

"Copy that," Grace said. His voice was as hard as granite, but she knew where to spot the glimmer of hope in his eye.

He rose to his feet with little difficulty, as if Libby weighed no more than a sack of sponges. "I'll take her downstairs and run the usual tests. You go out to the trailer and figure out what's going on with Nelson."

She held up her hands. "Nothing would make me happier than taking that bastard for a ride on the Pain Train. But if it's information you're after, you know I'm not much of a diplomat."

"Good point. Have Mr. Guillermo meet you there. He'll have everything you need for a proper…ah, summit."

"Not Cooper?" she asked. "I mean, I'm sure A.J. *could* do it, but Cooper has actually handled hostile interrogations before. Wouldn't he be a better fit to take the lead?"

"Normally, yes. But as you may recall, the Lieutenant is still on restricted duty after his encounter last week, and I doubt last night's antics helped his condition."

He had a point. Between the stab wound from a scythe-wielding man-lion and facing down a twenty-foot centipede-witch, Cooper had earned a break, and A.J. was perfectly capable. No logical reason to feel disappointed at all.

She tipped her chin at the battered car. "I assume you have a plan for this?"

John shrugged. "No one's going to give a tiny smash-up like this much attention, assuming anyone even comes this way today at all. We'll leave it for now. Perhaps Mr. O'Bannon can get it running long enough to drive it into the delivery bay when he gets in tonight."

"Copy that." She unwound Cari's house key from the ring and pocketed it. Her eyes wandered from the broken car to the bloodied woman, then back to John. "By the way," she said as she tucked the keyring into his hand, "that strange stuff we were supposed to keep an eye out for? I think we may have found it."

Chapter Two

Cari's knees felt like pudding and numbness dulled her thoughts. At least the myopic fury that had consumed her in the trailer was gone. She'd felt it flare up when she saw her mother hit the ground, but Rex's hand on her arm had snuffed it out. His touch penetrated the fog, light but steady on her right shoulder, as he guided her past the lockers and into the bunker.

"How 'bout a cup of Joe?" he practically yelled, steering her into the kitchen so quickly his toes caught the back of her sneakers and she nearly fell over. Behind them, John's body-laden steps thunked in the opposite direction.

She spun out from Rex's grip and tore after him.

"Mayhem, wait!" Rex called after her.

She didn't listen as she rushed past the entryway toward the holding cells. Out the corner of her eye she glimpsed Holly crushing herself against the bars of her own cell, her beady black eyes practically popping out of her head as they tried to follow John down the hall. Cari blinked, and Holly disappeared. All she saw now were the slim, swaying arms and legs that hung limply from either side of John's wide frame.

"I want to see her!" she wailed.

John paused in front of the second cell on the left but didn't turn around. "I can't let you do that, Cari."

White-hot rage filled her. She bobbed to the right, attempting to sweep around him, but John pivoted left and blocked her.

"Mr. Mackie, Cell Two!" The bars in front of him slid back and he plunged into the room. Before she could rush in after, a slim hand wrapped around her wrist and held her back.

"Let me go!" She wrenched against Rex's grip.

"No can do," he said, grunting as he struggled to hold on to her flailing limb. "You don't need to see that."

"Yes, I do!" she screamed in frustration as the bars slammed shut. "I want to see my mom!"

"She's not your mother!"

John's words froze her to the core. He finished securing his burden to the cot in the middle of the room and turned to face her, his body strategically positioned to block her view.

"She's not your mother," he repeated. "Not right now. I'm going to do everything I can to get her back for you, but until I do, it's best if you stay away. The first sedative is going to wear off soon, and when she wakes up, I'd like to keep her as calm and unstimulated as possible. You're the last person she should see."

The words stung like a hoard of bees, painful and burning. She had a right to be there, to stay by her side and see her through this. But John had put on his vacant, self-assured doctor face, the one that reminded her of the marble statues of Socrates and Plato staring up from the pages of her long-abandoned textbooks. She sulked in defeat. All the screaming in the world wouldn't do any good—there was no arguing with a stone. "Can you at least tell me how she is, *Doctor*?"

"When there's something to report, you'll be the first to know. I promise."

"Great," she snarled and stalked back to the kitchen, Rex at her heels.

"Sorry about that, May," he mumbled sheepishly as she slumped into a chair. "That dude is kind of dick, but in this case, he probably knows what he's talking about."

"Whatever," she snapped before inserting the tip of her thumbnail between her teeth and biting down angrily. Maybe Rex had been trying to help, but that didn't mean she was going to forgive him for being John's co-conspirator.

"Uh, well, why don't you just sit there and try to chill out and…watch me make the coffee?" He turned and busied himself at the counter.

As reluctant as she was to heed any instruction he gave her, her eyes followed along as he filled the pot with water and dumped it in the back chamber, then grabbed the filters from the upper shelf. Gradually the tense muscles in her neck started to loosen, and she let her hand fall back onto the table.

The nascent serenity was shattered by a furious scream, followed by a cascade of Holly's sadistic laughter.

Rex yelped. The coffee filters went flying as he twisted the knob on the coffee grinder. "Fresh beans!" he yelled over the roar of the gears. "Nothing better than fresh beans, that's what I say!"

As usual, Rex had all the subtlety of a Mack truck. A wave of appreciation swept over her, and she had to take several deep breaths to keep the hysterical giggles from tumbling out. Looking down, she saw her hands clenching the edge of the table so tight her knuckles were white. Her eyes welled, not with tears of sadness or worry, but guilt. She could've made a break for her mom's cell if she wanted to. Rex was slower than she was. He wouldn't be able to stop her. But she'd held herself in place with all her strength instead.

Because she didn't really want to see her mother. She just wanted to know that everything was going to be okay.

They'd been right to stop her.

The grinder ran until the hopper emptied, and beyond. Almost a full minute. By the time Rex shut it off, the disturbance down the hall had faded. She shoved her hands in the front pouch of her sweatshirt and focused on Rex's hands, dipping and waving like a magician as they performed their tasks. She closed her eyes. The next thing she knew, the smell of roasted chicory wafted across her nose.

"Here we go." Rex placed a mug in front of her. "What do you need? Cream, sugar…Xanex, maybe?"

"Black is fine."

He arched an eyebrow in surprise but said nothing, scooping three mountains of sugar into his own coffee before settling into the chair across from her.

"So…um, how are you doing?"

She bit her lip. They both knew it was the dumbest question ever in the circumstances. Still, he cared enough to ask it. For that, she owed him an honest answer.

"I'm scared."

He nodded solemnly. "Me too."

There was something on his mind, she could tell. Letting the silence sink in, she brought the mug to her lips. The coffee smelled like a house fire and tasted like burnt chalk, but she would endure it for as long as it took him to get the words out.

"You killed a guy with an ax today." He addressed the words to the tabletop.

She sighed, running her finger around the smooth ceramic lip. "I didn't kill him. I threw an ax at his face and the blade got lodged in his skull."

"That's usually the same thing."

"Not this time." She downed the contents of her cup in a single gulp. It wasn't so bad if you drank it fast enough.

"Still." He squirmed in his seat. "Are you…are you sorry you did it?"

"No."

She surprised herself at how quickly she answered. That's not what a normal person would do, would they? A normal person would at least feel somewhat conflicted about striking to kill, even if it was in self-defense—or in the defense of another, as it happened in this case. But as soon as the word flew from her lips, she knew she'd never said anything more honest in her life. "I'm not sorry I did it, and I don't feel bad at all."

She pushed her empty cup toward him.

"More coffee, please."

Chapter Three

Grace jogged to her car, her phone bobbling in her hand as she swiped through her contacts for A.J.'s number. He answered on the fourth ring.

"Hola?"

"I need you to meet me at Four Winds as soon as possible."

"Why, what's—?"

"A summit. I assume you know what that means."

"Dios mío." He sounded as if he'd been punched. *"Okay, I'm on my way."*

"Trailer Three. See you soon."

She hung up and selected another contact from the list. It barely rang once.

"Edensgate Security Office. Simon Mackie speaking."

"It's me. Has John briefed you on the situation?"

He snorted. *"If you're talking about the second rotting corpse now stinking up our holding cells—"*

"Her name is Libby." She cut him off with a snarl. "She's Cari's mom. Libby is her name. Understood?"

"Oh, r-r-right." Simon stammered. *"C-c-copy that. Sorry."*

"I'll let you make it up to me." Grace dug in her pocket for her keys. "I need you to get me some background on a local man. First name Nelson, last name Baines. Bravo, Alpha, India, November, Echo, Sierra. Got it?"

"Baines with a Bravo, 10-4," came the answer, followed by the chatter of computer keys. *"Anything specific you're looking for?"*

"Anything specific would be great," she said as she fastened her seatbelt.

"Roger. I'll call you when it's done. And…Grace?"

"Yeah?"

"Try not to do anything…you know, too stupid."

She smiled. "Thanks pal. Talk to you soon."

Grace burned rubber through town, slowing down only when the wobbling metal archway to Four Winds came into view. She entered the trailer park with the engine running at a low purr and cut the wheel to the right. The VW Bug lurched over the uneven mounds of dirt that served as a combination yard-driveway in front of the first trailer. Luckily, it appeared to be abandoned, as did many of the units near the entrance. When the mine kicked, the trailer park had expanded away from the road to accommodate all the citizens who could no longer afford the upkeep of their cushy in-town McMansions. Only the true hard cases still occupied the small, dumpy front units.

She spurred the vehicle toward the narrow thicket at the edge of the park and wedged it between a pair of spindly bushes, hoping the minty green paint job would help it blend into the scenery. She continued on foot, keeping to the tree line until she reached Cari's trailer. A perimeter check confirmed all windows were intact, and the door remained latched. Leaning against the rear wall, she released a tense, shaky sigh. She might not have the What or Why on Nelson, but at least she had a reasonable expectation of Where.

Before the morning air had time to chill her to the point of shivers, the crunch of heavy tires broke the silence. Peeking around the edge of the trailer, she spotted A.J.'s mud-splattered Jeep Cherokee rolling down the center drive. His head swiveled to either side like a surveillance camera until he caught sight of her. She rounded the trailer to meet him as he pulled in behind it, killed the engine, and hopped out. He wore his typical ensemble: black shirt, black jeans, boots, and duster. Everything except his cowboy hat. His salt-and-pepper hair fell across his forehead in wet, freshly showered strands, and his stubble was no less prominent than it had been a few hours ago.

"Feel like telling me what this is all about?" he asked, dark eyes brimming with concern.

Keeping her voice low, Grace filled him in on the events of the morning, from Ray's passing to Cari's return to the state of Libby Hembert—or what was left of her, anyway. A.J. nodded along, hands perched on his hips, his face as still as sandstone. It was only when she told him about Nelson's reported behavior that his forehead started to pinch, and his lips looked as if he'd sucked on a lemon.

"You're sure this all happened outside of Edensgate?" he asked, a subtle but distinct tremor in his voice.

"Simon's checking on Baines's history now, but as far as we know he's had no significant contact with the mall or anything in it."

He stared at her, eyes sloped and pleading, as if begging her to say it ain't so. She looked away, back toward the trailer—and saw the corner of one of the drawn shades flutter.

She smiled. "What say we go ask him ourselves?"

They circled around to the front door, pressing their backs to the trailer wall so they couldn't be seen from the windows. A.J. went up the stoop first, examining the door as Grace waited on the ground.

"Should be easy enough." He reached inside his duster and produced a rubber-handled stiletto knife, which he passed down to her, then turned his body perpendicular to the door and put his fists up. "You might want to stand back. There could be shrapnel."

"Easy, Chuck Norris." Grace held up the house key Cari had given her. "No need to wake the neighbors."

A.J. pouted but dropped his hands. "Fine. It's a shame though—my high kick is a thing of beauty."

"I'm sure it is," she murmured as she slipped past him. To her surprise, the key turned fluidly in the rusted-out lock. She glanced over her shoulder. "I'm left. You're right."

He nodded and assumed a runner's stance. From beneath his coat he produced a second stiletto and held it point forward, ready to impale.

She opened the door a crack, her body tense and ready for an onslaught.

"And...go!"

She charged inside. Her eyes sprinted over the bottle-littered table, then darted left, searching the fouled kitchen and narrow hallway for movement. Nothing. She whipped right. Also nothing, except A.J.'s back as he performed a similar sweep of the small living area.

"Clear?" he hissed back at her.

"Clear." Squinting in the unlit space, she examined her side of the trailer more carefully. "There's a couple closed doors down this way though."

"Yeah, I've got one on this side too."

Which window had been the one with the fluttering shade? She tried to picture it, but the vinegary stink of old wine made it difficult.

"Yours first," she said at last.

They shuffled down the narrow walkway between two tattered banquette couches, A.J. on tiptoe while Grace slid flat-footed in reverse, her eyes pinned to the opposite side of the trailer, until she bumped up against him.

"On a three count," he said. "Uno. Dos. *Très*!"

She turned around as his foot connected with the flimsy door in a powerful thrust that was, in fact, quite beautiful.

What they found on the other side of the door, however, was the exact opposite.

A cheap dresser and vanity took up space to the left and right of the door, both made of the same fake-wood veneer and piled high with what could only be called "sex junk:" a plastic feline face mask, five or six pairs of lace panties in a variety of Day-Glo stripper colors, half-melted candles, and a dozen or so empty flask-shaped bottles. But the truly unsettling part of the room was the bed. Except for two pairs of fuzzy pink handcuffs hanging on either side of the wrought-iron headboard, it was bare. No pillows or blankets, not even a fitted sheet, the satiny blue finish of the mattress dulled by a mottle of dingy brown stains. Most of them looked like water damage except for the patchwork of smeary, mud-colored slashes across the upper middle of the mattress.

"Jesus." A.J. passed a hand over his forehead, chest, and shoulders. "What the hell went on in here?"

"I *do not* wanna know," Grace said, sweeping the room for their quarry. The furniture took up almost all the floor space, the bed frame appeared to have a solid base, and there were no other doors to indicate a bathroom or closet. To see anything more would mean traversing that mattress, and she would rather set her hair on fire than get any closer to that abomination. She turned back toward the main room. "Come on, let's go check the other—"

Her words died. Outside the open bathroom door lurked Nelson, drooling and snorting like a bull.

At least, she assumed it was Nelson. It was hard to tell with the ax buried in the left side of his face. His once perfectly coiffed blond hair clung to his saggy cheeks, heavy with sweat, and his trim mustache was caked with gooey black blood.

"Graaaaaaace," he rasped, sinking into a low forward crouch.

Her vision tunneled as she cataloged the area between them. There was no alternate path, no room to maneuver, and no possible way to outflank him. At Edensgate, she could almost always count on at least one of those things. But here…

Her lungs evacuated as all further brain function came crashing to a halt. The hand holding the knife squeezed the handle in a death grip. If there was only one road to take, then why wait?

She sprang forward. He reeled back and pounced. A bound and a half later and she was close enough to smell the stink of alcohol oozing from his skin. His hands landed on her first. She heard the zip of fabric ripping as he clawed at her chest and shoulder. A picketed line of teeth hovered over her, white and black and red all over. That was it. A face and hands. The rest of him was hollowed out as he arched backward. Out of striking distance.

Her lips pulled back in a snarl. That son of a bitch meant to grab her, hold her, and rip her throat out, all without ever giving her an opportunity to counterattack.

Except...

The plan coalesced in her brain a half second before her body obliged. Turning her fist from a stab to a punch, she lashed out with a jab as beautiful as A.J.'s high kick, if not more so. When it landed, they both screamed: Grace from the impact that crushed her fingers and sizzled up her arm; Nelson from the additional inch and a half of ax blade she had drilled further into his skull. Grabbing his face, he collapsed to the floor.

Grace fumbled a dishtowel out from the refrigerator handle with fingers numb from the blow, then dropped down to straddle the drooling, whimpering man-demon. "What did you do to her?" she growled, twisting the towel between her hands.

Nelson giggled, gray spittle bubbling from between his clenched teeth. The edge of her vision turned red.

"Wrong answer, dick." She shoved the towel into his mouth and pressed the butt of her hand against the back of the ax. Another half-inch of blade disappeared into his face. He roared against the gag as more blood spurted from the wound in small, oily arcs. "Tell me what the hell you did to her!"

"Grace, stop!"

Strong, non-negotiable arms looped below hers and dragged her to her feet.

"He needs to tell us! I'll make him talk. Let me go!"

Her flailing arm smacked A.J. on the side of the head. He grunted, but his grip didn't weaken. "No, *querida*. Not like this. Now, be quiet. There's been enough screaming as it is."

She groaned, flopped her arms a few more times in protest, then gave in. A couple deep inhales of A.J.'s leather-polish-wildflower soap went a long way in cooling her fury.

"Better?" he asked as he withdrew his arms.

"I guess." She glared down at the bleeding, semi-conscious Nelson. "My way would have worked, you know."

A.J. indulged her with a smile. "Perhaps. But why don't we try the easy way first?"

Nelson wheezed something at them.

The fact that he thought he had the right to say anything without permission filled her with fresh rage. "*What* was that, asshole?"

His eyes fluttered and he whimpered again. A tenuous chain of words stumbled out of his semi-unconsciousness.

"Thank you…sir. Thank you."

A.J. swooped down and grabbed Nelson by the ankles, his eyes smoldering. "Give me twenty minutes. See how thankful you are then." He looked up at Grace. "Come. Help me drag this *pedazo de mierda* to the bedroom."

A.J. returned from the truck as Grace finished locking the second fuzz-covered metal cuff around an unconscious Nelson's left wrist. From the duffel bag in his hand, he extracted a length of rope and handed it to her. "Bind his ankles too. We need to restrict his movement as much as we can."

"It's your show, friend," she said, and looped the rope around Nelson's legs.

A.J. sidled around the right side of the bed and began unpacking the rest of the bag. She watched out of the corner of her eye as he laid a leather-covered blackjack on the dresser next to their two stiletto blades, followed by a crucifix, a syringe, a pair of pliers, what appeared to be a surgical-grade scalpel, and a whole host of other sharp and shiny implements.

"Are you really going to use all that?" she asked as she tied off the last knot.

"For the most part, no. It's psychological. If he's still any part human, it'll send a pretty loud message." He held up a handful of glass vials full of clear liquids with small, inscrutable writing, all identical except for the label color. "These, on the other hand, are our silver bullets, for when the conversation needs a jump-start."

"Uh-huh." Her task complete, she backed into the doorway. "You know what else makes a good silver bullet? An *actual* bullet."

"Perhaps. But threats of brute force could backfire depending on his state of being. Sometimes you need a more nuanced approach." He lined up the bottles on the dresser and pointed at the one with the green label. "Ketamine, to sedate and to relieve pain." Then the red label: "Platypus venom to bring that pain back times ten." Finally, the purple label: "Sodium pentothal, or what some call truth serum. Doesn't always work, but it rarely hurts...too much."

"Wow," she said, genuinely impressed. "And here I thought you were just the weapons guy."

"Knives and guns aren't the only weapons, Grace."

"No, but they are the best ones."

He smiled serenely. "We'll see."

The buzz of her phone sent her heart racing. "It's about time!" she said as she pressed the call button. "Simon. What have you got for me?"

"Quite a bit, actually. You ready for it?"

"One sec." She curled a finger at A.J., then stepped into the hallway. She was about to put the phone on speaker when A.J. stopped her hand.

"It's better if he doesn't know what we know," he whispered, tilting his head back toward the man shackled to the soiled mattress like a demented Jesus.

"Fair enough." She angled the phone upward so they could both hear. "Go ahead, Simon."

"Alright. Nelson A. Baines, born February 10th, 1971 at St. Agnes right here in Halcyon to Elizabeth and Abner Baines. He is the oldest of three. Sister Felicia was born 1973, and brother—"

"We don't need the family tree." A.J. cut him off before Grace could, and with a far less abrasive word choice. "Skip ahead to the last nine or ten years or so. What was he doing before the mine fell, and what has he been doing since?"

"One sec…okay, yes. He was head of security at First National Bank of Halcyon. When it shuttered in 2011, he got a job at the Stop-n-Go on the south side of town. His wife, Leeann, was and still is a Civics teacher at Halcyon High. He's got two kids, both girls. Kate, 17. Chloe, 15. Kate's on the basketball team at HHS, and might have a decent shot at a scholarship next year. Otherwise, college isn't looking good for either of them, according to their report cards."

"How did you get access to their report cards?" Grace asked.

"Uh…do you really want me to answer that?"

She smirked. "Withdrawn. Keep going."

"*Nelson worked at the S-n-G for about three years, then quit to devote all his time to his community outreach. Property records indicate that the family sold their house and moved to Four Winds around that time as well. Number #17, a triple-wide on the back hill overlooking the river. I guess he's the type that needs to have the nicest house on the block, even in a trailer park.*"

Grace nodded along. "And when you say, 'community outreach,' you mean his substance group-slash-circle jerk?"

"I think you mean prayer circle," A.J. corrected.

"I know what I mean," Grace shot back. "Simon?"

"*Uh, he does run a prayer* circle *and substance support group…in theory. But the only record I could find connecting him to any church is from before 2011, when he was a deacon at Our Lady of the Mountains. Since then he's had no affiliation with any church in town, and his group isn't listed on any event calendars. They have a single-page website that says they meet at seven every night, and it gives Nelson's house as the address, but other than that I haven't found any employment records or volunteer sign-ups, and there's nothing in his bank accounts that would indicate a donation to—*"

"We get it," Grace said. "Considering Libby's alcohol addiction, I think we can safely assume that's where they met. Do you have a sense of when they started seeing each other *outside* the group?"

"*Negative.*"

"Dammit!" She caught A.J.'s reproachful glare and corrected herself. "Sorry, Simon. That's not your fault. Any adulterer with half a brain would be careful not to leave a paper trail—which in this case is appropriate, given that half his brain is—"

"*Anyway*," A.J. interjected. "Now we know that the mine fall impacted Nelson in an extreme way."

"Well, no shit." Grace rolled her eyes at him. "It's not like everyone else won a car and a trip to Bermuda. But he's the only one that's gone full-on Cocoa Puffs."

"Exactly my point. Simon, you said he worked at the bank?"

"Affirmative. And he was good at it too. Even got a commendation from the governor when he helped foil some crazy hacking attempt back in '08. I tell ya, under different circumstances I could picture us hiring this guy."

"Right," Grace said around clenched teeth. The idea of working with Nelson made her want to throw up.

"Simon," A.J. chimed in as she recovered, "can you tell if he was in the bank when the news of the mine hit town?"

"One second…hold on…yes! His work schedule has him opening the bank that morning."

"That's what I thought." A.J.'s brows joined over his angular nose.

"What?" Grace asked, covering the phone with her hand. "What does that mean?"

"The bank was the first place most people went after they heard the mine was dead. A big group showed up several hours before it opened. The employees didn't want to let them in, so they broke the windows and stormed the place. That's where the first fatalities occurred."

"First of many," Grace said bitterly, thanking her lucky stars that she'd already been at Edensgate when the week of violence had kicked off. "You think one of the settlers got a hold of him there?"

"I suspect he experienced a uniquely horrific trauma on that first day, and it has led to something worse. I can use that." He brushed her hand away from the microphone. "This has been helpful, Simon. *Gracias.*"

"Oh well...de nada."

She shook her head as A.J. returned to the bedroom and closed the door. *What a bunch of nerds.*

"Simon, one last thing. That Bible study thing he runs—do you have a member list for it?"

Simon whistled through his teeth. *"That's a little trickier. Substance support groups, religious or otherwise, don't take attendance or keep member lists. That's how they can use the 'anonymous' tag."*

She smiled. "I'm sensing a 'but' coming."

"Buuuut, this is Halcyon we're talking about. Playing Six Degrees of Separation never makes it past round two. Give me a few days. I'll find who was in that group."

"10-4," Grace acknowledged. "Thanks. Would you mind patching me through to John's phone? I want to give him the update."

"Sure thing. Stand by."

She sat down on the cracked leather couch as a series of beeps and buzzes disrupted the line.

"I'm afraid we have a situation, Mr. Baines."

She looked up as A.J.'s voice filtered in from the other side of the door. "One that involves you, and the woman who lives here, and now, unfortunately, me. We have a problem we need to solve, and to do so, I'm going to need your help." The rubbery snap of a medical glove punctuated his words.

"Ms. Henry?"

She dragged her attention back to the phone. "Hey, Boss. Wanted to let you know we've got Nelson restrained. And, good news: I don't see any indication that he left the trailer or had contact with anyone else since Cari left him."

"What's his condition?"

She cringed. "Yeah, that's the bad news. He's conscious, but his condition is…pretty much what Cari said it would be."

"And by that you mean…?"

"Demonically possessed with an ax in his head."

"I see." His voice tightened. *"And his chances of recovery?"*

"In the toilet."

"Understood."

The word sounded so heavy it hurt her back to hear it. "Anyway…how's Cari holding up?" She wanted to ask about Libby too, but she had a feeling she wasn't going to like the answer.

"As well as can be expected. She's in the break room with Mr. Ranganathan, playing some sort of pugilistic video game."

"Well, next time you see her, let her know that Nelson has been handled, and that she doesn't have anything to worry about."

"That…might be a bit premature."

She stiffened. "What do you mean?"

"If his chances are truly, quote-unquote, in the toilet, is it safe to assume there would be no benefit of further detainment, or awaiting a possible antidote?"

"Correct," she said, resisting the urge to comment further. Eight years of nothing but goose eggs and he still would not let go of that stupid antidote idea.

"In that case, he will need to be dispatched."

"Tell me something I don't know," she said with an irritated sigh. "We can handle it, Boss. We've both done the vanishing dance more than once."

"Your skills are not my concern."

He paused. A fresh surge of anxiety kicked her heartbeat into overdrive. He was choosing his words.

He only did that when he was about to deliver the worst news.

"It's like this," he continued at last. *"Nine times out of ten, when someone from Halcyon disappears, it's because they simply up and moved. They decided to try their luck somewhere else, and who could blame them? It's unfortunate they didn't say goodbye, but everyone understands. That's good for us, because when that tenth time happens, it's dismissed out of hand like all the rest. Nelson Baines, however…he was part of whatever fabric still makes up this community. He had status. He had a family. When someone like that goes missing, people notice. They ask questions—and they will aim their suspicions at whoever saw him last."*

Grace did her best to suppress a shiver. "Simon didn't find any records that tie Nelson to Cari, and his affair with Libby was a secret, and a very well-hidden one it looks like. There's no reason anyone would think he was here last night."

"That's something at least," John said. *"But prying eyes don't always make the front page. Sometimes you don't know who saw what until it's too late."*

She rubbed her temple. "If we can't dispatch him, and we can't keep him alive, then what the hell *are* we supposed to do with him?"

"As I said, your skills are not my concern. I'm sure you will find the perfect solution."

"Thanks for the vote of confidence," she sniped. "I gotta go. I'll call when we have more."

"Thank you. And be careful."

The call cut out. She sat there for a moment, staring at the raggedy banquette across from her and wondering what she had been thinking when she had answered her landline that morning. After a moment she groaned, slapped her knees, and hauled herself up to stand. Might as well give A.J. the good news.

"Don't feel like talking?" His slow, deep baritone stopped her outside the door. "Given the headache you must have I can't say I blame you. What do you say I help you out with that, and then we can try again?"

Nelson's gagged screams shook the trailer to its metal bones. She opened the door as A.J. wrenched the ax from Nelson's face.

"Hey! You busy?"

"Marginally." He joined her at the foot of the bed. "What's the news?"

"Not much. John has every faith in us, he's looking forward to hearing what we discover—oh, and we can't dispatch him."

He stared at her as if she had told him it was currently raining ketchup. "But we can't keep him alive."

"I am aware of that."

"*Mierda.*" He tossed the blood-greased blade at Nelson's feet and rubbed his forehead in frustration. "You know who we could really use for this?"

Grace held up a warning finger. "Uh-uh. Don't even think about it. We are not to get him involved. Boss's orders."

They turned to the shivering creature strapped to the mattress. His tar-black eyes roamed over A.J.'s tools, the blades and bottles a stark omen of vicious things to come. The injured side of his face tilted skyward, revealing the cleaved flesh of his cheek. But it wouldn't stay that way for long. The wound had already started to suture itself, forming a jagged line of black jelly from the middle of his cheek to his eyebrow. A small bulge in the ocular cavity indicated a growing eyeball.

"Huh." A.J. tilted his head and frowned. "That's strange."

"Is it?" Grace asked over the buzzing of her phone. Unknown Number. She pressed the button to silence it. "Cari split his melon and a few hours later he's up and at 'em and trying to eat me for breakfast. Regeneration isn't that surprising."

"That's not what I mean." He turned his head slowly to either side, as if looking at Nelson from a slightly different angle would reveal the answer. "I have the strangest feeling that I've met him somewhere before. And not that long ago, either. Somewhere…" He trailed off, his expression befuddled and annoyed.

"It's a small town," she supplied. "We've probably both seen him dozens of times and not even—"

Her phone buzzed again. Unknown Number again.

"Do you need to take that?" A.J. asked.

She smirked. "As critical as my opinion is, I'm sure the Green Wind Initiative will survive without it." She hit decline, then silenced her phone. "Sorry about that."

"*De nada.* We should probably get started though. There's a lot of ground to cover, and I don't want to find out what happens to this *monstruo* once it gets dark."

Chapter Four

Rex mashed the buttons of his controller. A series of audio embellishments whooshed from the television, punctuated by some ninja-esque exclamations. On the screen across from the couch, a frog and a gorilla dressed in *gi* and headbands tossed each other around in a Technicolor blur.

"Watch this, Mayhem! I got him now."

Cari lifted her head from the arm of the couch, attempting to feign interest. She'd been watching Rex play for hours, and her eyes throbbed.

"Dammit!" Rex yelled as the gorilla grabbed the frog by its ankles and tossed it into a rock wall at the back of the playing field.

"And *boom* goes the dynamite!" Simon's scruffy, triumphant grin replaced the combat on the screen. "Give it up, young Padawan. You cannot defeat the master."

"Lucky shot." Rex pouted, rolling his thumbs over the joysticks impatiently. "Best of twenty-one."

"If you insist. Get ready to be owned once again."

"You wish." Rex thrust his chin at the spare controller on the table. "You sure you don't want to play, May?"

"No, thanks." Her legs ached as she slid off the couch. "I think I'm gonna go for a walk."

He tore his eyes off the selection screen to look at her. She shrank away from the worry creasing his face. "You, uh, want me to come with?"

"No, that's okay," she said quickly as she hurried away. "I just...want to be alone for a minute."

She dashed out of earshot before he could say anything else. It wasn't that she didn't appreciate the offer. But his desperation to paint this as a "a normal day" had begun to grate on her nerves. Nothing about this was normal, and she feared she might start clawing her skin off if she had to pretend it was for one more second.

When she reached the lockers, she slowed to a shuffle, letting her attention wander down the hallway toward the detention cells. Her ears strained to catch any noise. More specifically, she listened for words, or even intelligible grunting—anything that resembled human communication. Instead, she could only make out the occasional click of metal on metal and a shivering but steady breath.

"He won't save her."

The words swooped in from out of nowhere, piercing her skin and filling her veins with fire.

"And how would you know?" she snapped at the barred door of Cell One.

Holly giggled. She sat on the floor, her back pressed tight against the wall and her legs splayed long across the stained concrete. Milky gray eyes rolled in their sockets, and everything else had taken on a slightly seaweed tone, from her ragged skin to her matted blond hair, even her tattered jeans and blouse. She looked dried out, like a husk ready to crumble at any moment. Everything except for her mouth, where her perpetually splitting lips oozed brown fluid like self-renewing lip gloss.

"I know," she croaked, prompting another micro-split in her bottom lip, "because of *who* did it to her."

"I was there." Cari lowered her voice to a whisper and tiptoed closer to the cell, shooting a glance down the hall as she did so. She had a feeling John wouldn't like her talking to Holly. "I saw Nelson do it."

Holly rolled her head side to side and hacked out another chuckle. "You think because you and your friends beat back the waves night after night that makes you safe? We made this place. We are the eyes in the trees, the shadows and the light, the water and the sand. We are the soul of Halcyon, and that can never be undone. Not by you, or them, or anyone."

"Then why are you all still here?" Cari sneered. "If you're so big and tough, you should be able to flick us aside and walk out the front door. Instead, you lose. Night, after night, after night."

Holly growled and slammed her skull back against the blocks. The resulting crack made Cari reel back.

"Maybe we're a little…waylaid, at the moment." Her eyes narrowed with vicious delight. "But who's to say that some impotent little morsel didn't break free, and find a cozy nook somewhere to squirrel away in, all coiled up like a rattlesnake, waiting until the time is right?"

Cari bit the inside of her cheek to suppress a shiver. "*Is* that what happened?"

Holly closed her eyes as a dark liquid dribbled down the wall behind her head. "If it did, then the best case for Mommy is becoming our new roommate."

The blood-slathered smile widened. "Actually, that's not true. Her best case is to die."

"I don't believe you," Cari spat.

"Don't you?" Her eyes slipped halfway open. "She's still in here, you know. Your little boss lady."

The shock of the words froze Cari to the core. "She is?"

"Oh, yes. She resisted at first, but eventually she saw it was the only way." She tilted her head, her face a mask of innocent curiosity. "Would you like to know if she wishes you had killed her?"

Cari's body trembled as cold fear battled hot rage. Holly hadn't been a good boss, or even a particularly nice person, but she hadn't been all bad—definitely not bad enough to justify this. She wanted to strangle whatever it was that now wore her skin. Instead, she bolted, dashing past the lockers and up the stairs to the main floor.

She would not give it the satisfaction of seeing her cry.

Chapter Five

Grace shifted her weight from foot to foot as a bead of sweat trickled down her spine. The cramped little room had grown hot, humid, and was starting to stink. She'd been standing at the foot of the bed for what felt like years, observing as A.J. plied Nelson with questions about his relationship with Libby. But Nelson just grunted and shook his head, his mouth a tense, uncooperative line.

Then A.J. switched topics, and asked Nelson about the bank, and that horrible November morning when everyone discovered the mine had fallen. Nelson's face looked as if the bone below his milk-white skin had turned to jelly. His mouth sagged open, but no answers came out. Instead, he wailed and thrashed like a chained bull, spitting profanities and gray mucus and threats of what he would do to them as soon as he got free. The tantrum was no more productive than the silence, but at least grabbing Nelson's bound ankles while A.J. shoved the dishrag back in his mouth was something to do.

"Fine, then." A.J. huffed. Returning to the dresser, he picked up the syringe and stuck the needle into the green painkiller bottle, then the purple source of truth. "A little Good Cop, Sneaky Cop it is."

He plunged the needle into Nelson's neck, eliciting another shriek, albeit a stifled one.

"About damn time." Grace sighed with relief as Nelson's eyelids drooped and his frustrated noises turned soupy.

"There we go," A.J. cooed, removing the gag once again. "That's better, isn't it, Mr. Baines?"

Nelson's eyes twitched from A.J. to her. She stiffened, fighting the urge to recoil. Those bottomless eyes both disgusted and fascinated her, like twin voids she could get lost in.

"Let's start at the beginning." A.J. leaned back against the dresser. "Tell me about the bank."

Nelson uttered a noise like a rooting pig. His wrists flopped in their restraints.

"You were there the morning the mine fell, weren't you? What happened?"

Another deep-throated grunt, then silence.

A.J. sighed mournfully and retrieved the blackjack from the dresser. Her heart raced; finally, something she could help with.

"You need to cooperate with us, Mr. Baines," she chimed in. "It's for your own good."

Nelson turned his infinite stare back on her. "Fuck you, bitch."

A.J. brought the blackjack down hard on Nelson's left shin. The resulting crack suggested something had broken, and yet Nelson barely whimpered.

"Dammit," she said. "You gave him too much. How are we supposed to get answers if he can't feel anything?"

"Better than screaming loud enough to wake up the entire city. Besides, you're forgetting about the second part of that little cocktail." He resumed his stance by the dresser, slapping his palm with the business end of the baton. "Keep going."

She shrugged. This was A.J.'s circus. She was just one of his freaks.

"We know that there were at least ten people in the bank when the riot broke out, because that's how many were killed. Ten dead citizens, none of them you." She pressed both hands into the soiled mattress and leaned toward Nelson. "How did you escape?"

More snarling, but still no answers.

"Did someone help you, Mr. Baines? Did you have an accomplice? A partner?"

He bucked violently, as if her words were red-hot whips, sucking in breath through clenched teeth. He'd wrenched so hard against his cuffs that black blood had begun to seep from his wrists, soaking the fuzzy pink marabou lining the handcuffs. She grinned. They had him, like a bug under glass, A.J.'s truth serum the pin keeping him in place. He could rip himself to pieces trying to resist, but there would be no wriggling away from this one.

"Who was it, Mr. Baines? Who helped you get out of the bank?"

His jaw popped in defiance as his clenched teeth parted, and the words he had tried so hard to contain spewed forth:

The Story does begin anew
When the Storykeeper dies
In the rosy dawn that follows
That unfortunate demise.

When the Primal Seal is opened
And the flowered sprite received,

The Flooded Prophet takes the throne
To avenge the much deceived.

He slumped back and let out a snotty sob of defeat.

A.J. cleared his throat. His face was stoic, playing it cool. But his eyes were a little too round, the knuckles of his hand clenching the blackjack a little too white. "That mean anything to you?"

"Not all of it," she muttered back. "Storykeeper was the Courier's name for Ray. I remember he called him that on the morning of the mine fall. The Storykeeper dies…and the rosy dawn that follows…that's today. A new story starts today."

"What does that mean?"

She shook her head and turned back to Nelson. "Mr. Baines, what story are you talking about? And what about the…the Primal Seal?"

"When the Primal Seal is opened," Nelson recited, his eyes ticking in time with the rhythm, "And the flowered sprite received the Flooded Prophet takes the throne to avenge the much deceeeeeeived…" The words died beneath a peal of wild laughter.

"Mr. Baines!" she shouted. "Stop that! Mr. Baines, can you hear me?"

The laughter escalated, creating a rubbery wall of noise that filled the room and pressed into her ears, threatening to break in and leech its poisoned madness into her brain.

Staggering back a step, she pointed at A.J. He leapt from the dresser and bashed Nelson twice across the mouth. The noise stopped immediately.

"Okay," she said, taking a breath to steady herself. "Let's try that again. When you said—"

He snapped his head up to look at her. "Have you ever been to hell?"

She couldn't do anything but stare at him in surprise. For a guy who'd been hit in the face twice, he seemed remarkably sharp. Now it was her turn to play it cool.

"Hell?" she mused, hooking her thumbs into the belt loops of her coveralls. "Yeah. Every damn night."

He giggled and dropped his head back to the mattress. "You think that puppet show is hell? Hardly. What you've seen is shadows on a wall. But all that is going to change. The Prophet has awakened. He will open the Primal Seal, and then...then you'll know the ultimate truth."

"And what is that?"

He shook his head. "You're not ready."

"Try me."

He tucked his chin and gave her another maggoty once-over. "Mankind has outlived its usefulness. We tell ourselves these grand myths about being created in God's likeness, but we're the cosmic equivalent of cockroaches. We foul everything we touch with our self-indulgence and greed."

Grace raised her eyes to the ceiling. "Oh, right. We're the disease, and you're the cure. But I'm curious—have you looked in a mirror lately? Because from where I'm sitting, you look a lot more plague-like than I do."

He scoffed as if in a world full of idiots, she was the Idiot Supreme. "I knew you wouldn't understand."

"You got me there. Who fed you this garbage? Was it this Prophet guy?"

He averted his eyes and studied A.J.'s arsenal. "No one needed to tell me. It's as plain as dirt."

She smirked. "Oh, I see. You've never met the Prophet, have you?"

"No," he sighed, his voice full of regret and longing. "But I will. Soon. He's coming, and when he arrives—"

"Yeah, yeah, ultimate truth and the destruction of all humankind. We got it. I don't suppose you know where this Primal Seal is, do you?"

He gurgled into his chest like a happy baby. "Even if I did, I wouldn't tell you."

"Don't play games with us, Mr. Baines. We have methods of making you speak," A.J. said in his best Russian accent as he stuck the syringe into the red vial and drew a full dose of the pain-magnifying liquid into the chamber.

Grace flicked her hand at him dismissively. "Don't bother."

He wrinkled his forehead in confusion. She raised her eyebrows, indicating he should follow her lead. "This moron is bottom-rung. He doesn't know anything."

Nelson looked as if she'd slapped him. His cheeks flushed and his eyes bugged with wrathful tears. "That's not true!"

"Sure, it is. I mean, all you've done so far is regurgitate some lame rhetoric and recite a poem that, frankly, my six-year-old niece could've written in her sleep." She looked back at A.J. "Kill him and let's get out of here."

"You're wrong," Nelson's voice shook as A.J. picked up the stiletto. "I was chosen."

"You're a shit pile, and you're wasting our time."

Taking the cue, A.J. lowered the point of the knife toward Nelson's shriveled right eye.

"I'm a shit pile?" Nelson screamed, his voice rising to the pitch of a teen-aged boy. "I'm a *shit pile*? Then why was I in charge of raising the army?"

"Hold it." Grace said before the point could pierce its target. She extended her hand to Nelson. "Go on."

"I-I-I don't know where the Primal Seal is," he stuttered, his focus on the point hovering mere inches from his face. "Only that it's difficult to get to. The Prophet wouldn't be able to get there without reinforcements. It was my job to find them."

Cold fingers tickled the back of her neck. "That's why your prayer circle wasn't associated with any church. You were using it as a cover to farm converts. Was Libby the first?"

He snorted. "She was supposed to be, until her little brat showed up and *ruined* it."

Grace leaned forward on her hands once again. "And why her? Why did you start the affair?"

He cocked his head almost ninety degrees and grinned at her. "Because I wanted to fuck her, of course."

She didn't even try to hide her disgust. "So, this is all a coincidence? You're just some horny asshole and banging Libby didn't have anything to do with Edensgate. Or with Cari."

"Mmmmm, Cari." A deep moan reverberated from Nelson's throat as if saying her name was pleasure itself. A pit of mortal dread sunk into Grace's stomach. "What do you want with her?"

She regretted her word choice instantly.

"Wouldn't you like to know?" He thrust his crotch in the air, the tip of his mottled gray and black tongue sliding over his lower lip.

She didn't remember moving across the room or picking up Cari's blood-smeared ax where A.J. had dropped it on the mattress. But both must have happened, because the next thing Grace knew, she was pressing that ax to Nelson's throat.

"You sick bastard."

"She'd *love* it!" His eyes slid to the right, away from her.

She grabbed the back of his neck and jerked his head upward. "Look at me, motherfucker! Look at me when I'm killing you!"

"Hang on a second."

"What?" she roared, ticking her gaze toward A.J.

He smiled thoughtfully, as if the final piece of an invisible puzzle had fallen into place. "I have something I need to ask him."

"He's tapped out! All he's got left is his twisted fantasies, and I'd rather rip my ears off—or *his*—than listen to that."

"You can do all the ripping and slicing and bashing you want in a minute. But one more question first."

"Fine," she growled, recoiling temporarily to the opposite side of the bed. "*One* more."

A.J. bent low, until his mouth was level with Nelson's face, and waited until the confined man turned his dark stare on him.

"What is your middle name?"

Nelson's wide black eyes widened even more, and he bared his teeth at A.J. "Go to hell."

Sighing, A.J. dug two fingers into the seam of Nelson's not-entirely healed face wound.

"Tell me," he coaxed, as composed as a librarian over Nelson's agonized screams. The answer came out in a long rasp, as if A.J. had reached all the way down his throat and ripped it out of him. "*Aaaaarrrrthhhhur.*"

A.J. retracted his hand. "Good boy."

He patted Nelson on the forehead, leaving a big black blotch behind.

Grace gaped at him. Had she heard that right? "Arthur. As in the *Reverend* Arthur?"

A.J. pried the soiled glove off his hand. "I guess we should have let Simon take the Baines family tree all the way to the roots after all."

"Guess so. How the hell did you know?"

"There's a family resemblance. The golden hair, the fatty jawline. The *presunción arrogante*. And Simon did mention his middle initial was A. But it was when he was looking at my tools that I first noticed it. He zeroed in on the crucifix like it was a picture of an old girlfriend - a combination of nostalgia, excitement, and shame."

He picked up the wooden cross and held it in front of Nelson. His eyes widened, enthralled, and his head lifted off the pillow as if it were magnetized.

"He looked at it every time he felt insecure or threatened. When we first tied him down, when he admitted he'd never met the Prophet, and when you had the ax on him now. That last is when it finally clicked." He tossed the cross back on the dresser. Nelson flopped onto the mattress, panting with exertion. "He's a member of the Reverend's progeny. His foulness would never allow him to look at a religious tool like that otherwise."

"I'll show you a religious tool," Nelson growled through a smarmy grin.

She cocked her eyebrow at A.J. "May I?"

He shrugged. "A deal is a deal."

Grace smashed the side of the ax into Nelson's skull. Black liquid spewed from his mouth as something snapped around his right temple and his chin sagged disjointedly on his chest.

"Anyway," Grace said over Nelson's agonized gurgles, "You think the Reverend's behind this somehow?"

"A blood connection *is* significant," A.J. mused. "And the timing works out. He was free for several hours before you and John trapped him at Edensgate after the initial deal expired, during which time Nelson managed to escape a massacre without a scratch." He shrugged. "It's not rock solid, but it' the best lead we've got."

"Works for me." She pulled out her phone. "Why don't you see if you can get any more out of Dickbrain here while I give John the update?"

"Sure. Mind if I wait until he re-hinges his jaw first?"

"Whatever makes your life easier."

As she retreated to the living room, she noticed a spring in her step that had not been there earlier. Not only had they identified the likely source behind Nelson's antics, it wasn't some crazy new monster after all. And…what was the saying? The devil you know, and so on. Sure, they were nowhere on that whole Storykeeper-Primal Seal-Prophet nursery rhyme, but if there was anything left to get (other than a bunch of old pervert BS), A.J. would surely get it out of him.

She was about to dial John's number when a new nightmare emerged: three short, decisive raps on the trailer door.

Busted.

Chapter Six

The twang of a country-rock guitar roused Cooper out of his semi-conscious haze. Fortune Son. He smiled and snuggled his pillow. That was his favorite song. He liked it so much he had made it his ring tone.

Ring tone…

Was his phone ringing?

He glanced at the nightstand, taking care not to disturb the sleeping woman draped over him. The only thing glowing was the illuminated 15:13 of the digital clock. He must have left his phone in the kitchen.

"Great," he grumbled, and forced himself up.

"Don't leave me," Allie murmured, wrapping her leg around his waist.

"It's my work phone."

"You're off the clock. Let it go to voicemail."

As if it had heard her, the song cut out.

"See? Problem—"

The riff began anew. Cooper's heart rate shifted into a higher gear. Back-to-back phone calls. Never a good sign.

"I *have* to answer. They'd only be calling me if it was important."

"So, some kids spray-painted boobs on the front doors again. Is that really more important than staying here with me?"

He sighed. "Of course not. But if I don't answer, it'll be in the back of my head all day. How will I be able to give you my undivided attention?" He pressed his mouth into hers until she moaned with pleasure, then quickly pulled away, grinning. "See? I can't concentrate."

"Tease." She unwound her limbs and shoved him playfully toward the edge of the bed. "Fine, go. I hope it's worth it."

He dashed down the stairs, pulling on boxers as he went. The row of wounds that ran along the inside of his calves and thighs throbbed with every movement, but he ignored them. The pain was a mere fraction of what it had been when he'd arrived home that morning and improving by the minute. Apparently, being skewered by the feet of a giant demon centipede sounded a lot worse than it was.

He snatched the phone from the kitchen table. "O'Bannon."

"Coop? Thank God! It's about frigging time."

The voice was a little deeper and a lot rougher than last time—she must have started smoking again—but he recognized it instantly. "Lola?"

"Yeah, it's me. Sorry to call on your work phone, but it's the only number I've got for you."

"No, no, not a problem." He sat down at the table. Her voice conjured an image of Ray, smiling and congenial as always—at least, before he'd gotten sick.

"I'm so sorry about your dad. How are you holding up?"

"No offense, but can we do the whole condolences thing later? I'm afraid I've got a bit of…an emergency?"

He smiled at the tablecloth. "Sure. Is there an issue with your flight? Was it delayed or something?"

"What flight?"

"Your mom told Allie that you were flying home from Honolulu today."

Silence.

"Actually, Cooper, I'm already here. Well, I'm in LA. I fly to San Francisco tonight and then I'll take a shuttle the rest of the way at first line. But I've been stateside since yesterday."

His thoughts stumbled, then righted themselves. "Oh, of course. You flew out when you heard your dad was admitted. Your mom must have gotten it mixed up."

Another long silence. *"You know that's not what happened. Though maybe it should have been. Mom's been calling me every other day for a month, telling me he was getting worse. I swear, I meant to plan a trip. But as soon as I hung up, it all sort of…faded away. And then yesterday, the whole thing hit me so hard I damn near fell out of my chair in the middle of a packed elevator. It wouldn't leave me alone after that, just kept pounding in my head like a heartbeat. Come, home. Come, home. On and on until I booked my flight. Fucking Halcyon."* She chuckled. *"But I don't need to tell you about that, do I?"*

Cooper bit the inside of his lip. Time to change the subject. "So…if it's not a problem with your flight, what is it? Whatever you need, I'm here. Allie and me both."

"Oh, yes!" she cried. *"I need to find Grace, but she's not answering her phone. Do you know where she is?"*

Cooper frowned. Had Lola ever met Grace? When would that have been? He racked his brain for memories of them together and came up blank.

"Hello?"

"I'm here. Sorry. Last I saw her she was heading home. It was…kind of a rough night. She's probably asleep."

"Cooper." The deepening of her voice on the second syllable told him to cut the BS. *"You and I both know that's a ridiculous statement. Now stop trying to make me feel better and help."*

"Yes, ma'am." He smiled as an image of her in high school floated in front of him: long, stick-straight black hair framing her pale round face, her almond eyes and down-turned lips both smeared with black stuff that made the unamused stares she gave him even more intimidating. And while a devastating car wreck had left her body paralyzed from the waist down, the spirit he'd grown up with remained as bright and terrifying as ever. "I'll do a roll through town to see if I can find her."

"And call me as soon as you do?"

"The very minute. Don't worry. You just get here safe, okay?"

She laughed bitterly. *"Cooper my man, that's one thing I don't think I have to worry about."*

He shivered. She was probably right. What Halcyon wanted, it got. No exceptions, no substitutions, no delays.

After they said goodbye, Cooper took a shot at Grace's numbers himself. The home line rang endlessly, and while her cell phone didn't go straight to voicemail, it got there eventually. He sighed and bounded up the stairs. It seemed he was in for an afternoon of wild goose chasing—or rather, Grace-chasing.

Allie sat up as he entered the bedroom. "Who was it?"

"Lola," he said, swiping his balled-up work slacks from the floor. "She's…about to board the plane."

"Oh, good!" Allie sighed. "It'll be good for her to come home for a while. Her and Mimi both."

"Sure." He pulled on his pants, wishing he could share his wife's confidence. "Anyway, she called to ask for a favor, so I've got to run out for a while."

Her brows tightened. "Now? She's not even on the plane yet. What's the rush?"

"She needs to get a hold of Grace and can't find her. I promised I'd track her down."

"So, what? You're going to drive around town and hope you run into her?"

"I'll check her house and the mall first. Otherwise, yeah. Pretty much."

"That's insane."

"The town isn't that big. It won't take long."

"No, I mean…" Allie stared at her knees. "Look, you know I love Grace. But you're not her babysitter. If she's not answering her phone, it means exactly what it means when any adult doesn't answer their phone: she wants to be left alone."

"She might be in trouble."

"How?" Allie threw her hands up. "Has she been kidnapped by terrorists? Is she hanging off a cliff by her fingernails? No. That kind of stuff never happens here."

He pulled a maroon sweatshirt over his head and knelt to lace up his boots. Technically, it was true. *That* kind of thing never did happen.

"I'll be back as soon as I can." He stood up and dropped a kiss on top of Allie's tousled raven hair. She clutched his sleeves, holding him in place despite his attempts to pull away.

"Please. Please don't leave me."

He smiled, projecting patience. "I know you're still shook up about Ray. But Lola needs me."

"*I* need you." She pouted in that spoiled little girl way that always made him cringe. Summoning every ounce of tenderness he could, Cooper cupped her cheek in one hand.

"I know you do, sweetheart," he said, trying to keep his jaw loose and unclenched. "I'll tell her to charge her phone, then I will be right back here. It won't be more than an hour, at most."

"Promise?" she asked.

His skin crawled as her pronunciation tickled at the edge of "pwomise."

"Yes, I...*promise.*"

"Okay." She tucked her chin into his palm and smiled. "I *wuv* you."

He kissed her then, as much to smother any more of that shudder-inducing baby-talk as to say goodbye.

Maybe even more so.

Chapter Seven

Nelson's head snapped up at the knock on the trailer door. He opened his mouth, but A.J. shoved the towel gag between his lips before he could utter a single screaming syllable. With the prisoner subdued, A.J. joined Grace in the hall.

"What do we do?" he whispered, pulling the bedroom door closed behind him.

Grace's mouth fell open, but no words emerged. Her brain felt like it had short-circuited. "Maybe...look and see who it is first?"

He edged passed her and peered out the small, smudged window over the sink.

"It's some lady. Blond, forties. *Terrible* jean jacket." He wrinkled his nose in disgust. "I thought we all agreed bedazzling ended in the nineties."

"Do you recognize her?"

He looked as if she'd requested that he drink from the toilet. "Bitch, do I *look* like I hang out with the Rhinestone Housewives of Storey County?"

"Bitch, it was only a question," Grace said with a giggle, as amused as she was surprised. "Think you can take the attitude down a notch?"

"Lo siento." He pressed a hand to his chest. "It's that jacket. Apparently, bedazzle is a trigger for me."

"I'd say so. Let's be quiet, and maybe she'll go away."

They settled into the silence. Each knock-free second that passed buoyed Grace's spirits.

She's about to leave. Any minute now.

"Some folks are born, silver spoon in hand…"

They both stared in horror as Cooper's CCR ring tone belted from the phone in her hand.

"Fuck!" she hissed as she fumbled to hit Decline. *Maybe she didn't hear that. Maybe she'll think it was the radio. Maybe—*

"I know you're in there, Libby!" The thick Southern accent shivered the thin walls. "Open this door right now!"

A.J. groaned. "I don't think she's leaving."

Grace glared at him. "You don't know that for sure."

"I'm not leaving!" A flurry of knocks ensued that, if left unchecked, would probably shake the flimsy door right off its hinges.

"You were saying?"

"Fine," Grace grumbled, weighing the options. Indignance wouldn't work. Whoever this woman was, she seemed to know who lived here and who didn't. Getting aggressive would only make her suspicious—or worse, provoke her into calling the cops. But it didn't sound like she was in the mood to be soothed either. Which left only one option. A risky one, but the best they had.

"Okay, I got this." Grace ripped the handkerchief off her head and dug her fingers into her thick black curls, making them look as unkempt as she could. Then she unzipped her coveralls.

"Are you planning to…seduce her?" A.J. asked, his eyebrow arching higher with each movement.

"Not exactly." She knotted the sleeves at her waist. Her dingy white tank top looked bright against her sienna skin. "You hide behind the door. If anything goes wrong, I'll signal for help."

"How?"

"I'll say 'bedazzle.' Then you jump in and scratch her eyes out. Sound good?"

He eyed her viciously. "*Eres la peor, mi amiga.*"

She winked at him as he tucked himself between the jamb and the counter. With one more bracing breath, she plastered on a Miss America smile and flung the door open.

"Well, hi there!" she effused in an accent even thicker than the stranger's own.

The woman recoiled. She was about Grace's height, but so thin and delicate Grace thought she could probably carry her on one shoulder. Her bleached hair fell to her shoulders in feathered waves. And the jacket…it wasn't just bedazzled, it was be*crusted*. How A.J. knew there was jean under all those blue, pink and gold sequins, Grace had no idea.

The woman scanned Grace's hair, face and body with increasing concern. "Who in Hades are you?"

Grace popped out her hip and raised her chin in a still-cordial-but-slightly-affronted pose. "I don't reckon that's any of your business, ma'am."

"My name is Leann Baines. I'm looking for—"

"Oh, my word!" She slapped her knee in fake exuberance. "You're Nelson's wife! Oh, Libby is always goin' on and on about what a blessin' he's been. I don't know if you know this, but my sister is afflicted with a bit of a…temperance problem. Your husband has been an absolute angel, helpin' her like he has."

"Uh…oh, I see," Leann said through an uncomfortable frown. "So, your Libby's—"

"Sister. Yes, ma'am, as I said. Well, half-sister." She patted her hair. "Clearly."

Leann gulped, her cheeks flushing. "Uh…yes. Of course."

"Anyway, I'm afraid Libby's not here." Grace nodded at the tire tracks gouged in the dirt near the main drive. "She took the car into town a while ago. But you're more'n welcome to wait here if you'd like."

From behind the door, A.J. flashed her a look of alarm. But Leann already backed up another half step, her palms out as if the invitation were a raised fist. "No! No, that's not necessary. I was looking for Nelson, but I guess…maybe he's made his way back home by now."

"I reckon that's probably it, though I'm awful sorry to say it. I'd *love* to thank him for all he's done." Grace widened her smile. "Matter a' fact, would you mind tellin' him that when you see him? If it's not too much trouble, I mean?"

"Of course, I will." Leann stumbled backward down the steps and landed awkwardly on the ground. "Uh, thank you."

"No trouble at all. Y'all have a good day now!"

She watched Leann disappear around the back of the trailer before slamming the door.

A.J. smirked at her. "That was some accent. Dolly Parton would be proud."

"Thanks. West Virginia, born and raised."

"How did you know she wouldn't want to come inside?"

"Oh, you know. Women like that would rather peel their own skin off than share close quarters with…someone like me."

"Ah." He frowned. "Not exactly PC."

"Not exactly my fault." She smirked as she zipped up her coveralls. "Besides, it got rid of her, didn't it?"

He shrugged and smiled. "*Touché.*"

"Thank you." She lifted the blind on the window over the dining table, watching Leann as she tottered over the uneven ground toward the rear of the park and, Grace presumed, the big trailer with the river view. When the glint of the gaudy jacket faded behind the trees, she made her way back toward the bedroom. "Come on, let's snuff this candle before—"

Her voice fled the moment she opened the door.

Blood. So much blood, black and thick, soaking the blue satin mattress.

And…

"Where the fuck *is* he?"

She turned to A.J. His face had gone as pale as milk.

"It's…not possible." He shuffled toward the head of the vacant bed and poked at the handcuff with the tip of the blackjack, stooping to examine the blood-drenched metal-and-fur mechanism. "Locked. A little bent, maybe, but still, there's no way…"

Her body quaked with dread. *Of course, there was.*

She dove forward, but it was too late. Nelson's dismembered left hand leapt from its hiding spot behind the headboard and wrapped itself around A.J.'s throat. He stumbled backwards into the dresser, his mouth widening with a silent scream as he tried to pry the slick fingers from around his neck.

"Son of a bitch!" She dove for the arsenal laid out on the dresser, grabbing the first thing she saw: a pair of metal pliers. Yanking them wide open, she clamped down on the stumpy, tattered wrist and tugged as hard as she could. The deteriorating flesh tore instantly, spilling something like gray-green pudding down the front of A.J.'s chest. The stench of curdled milk and dirty diaper made her gag. But she held on, squeezing and ripping as more and more putrid ooze wept from the stump.

"It's...working," A.J. wheezed around the thing's weakening grip. "Don't...stop."

She nodded, wrenching as more and more of its insides plopped out.

Silver glinted to her right. She turned to see Nelson's other hand scurry down the front of the dresser, holding the scalpel between its index and middle finger like a cigarette.

"Fuck!" she screamed as the bladed appendage raced across the floor with spider-like speed. She barely managed to scramble onto the bed before it could take a swipe at her ankle.

"Grace..." A.J. coughed, sinking to his knees as Lefty renewed its hold around his neck. Even at this distance she could see the fingers begin to re-plump.

Fucking regeneration.

A rustle off the edge of the mattress drew her attention. Another surprise attack? Not very creative. Then again, brainless disembodied limbs weren't really known for their imagination.

Either way, two could play at that game.

"Hold on! I'm coming!" she yelled as loudly as she could (in case the thing has sprouted ears too) and launched forward.

The tiny assassin sprung upward as she crossed the edge of the bed. Just as she expected. Twisting her body away from the blow, she plucked the hand out of the air as easily as she would an apple from a branch.

"Hi there, little fella," she murmured, then turned her wrist and drove its scalpel into its brother's back. Lefty's fingers snapped open, relinquishing A.J.'s neck like a leech that had been doused in salt. A.J. gulped in air as his attacker fell to the ground, weak and impaled. Its custardy flesh ran out of the wound in a thick, ceaseless river.

Grace slammed Righty onto the dresser, picked up one of the remaining blades, and drove down, penetrating flesh and bone and particle board as she pinned the horrid creature to the veneer. It shuddered for a moment, then lay still.

A.J. looked down at the stinking gray smear on his shirt. He sneered down at the flaccid, trembling thing. "This was Ralph Lauren, you *cabrón*."

He dropped the heel of his boot onto the delicate knife and rubbery flesh, grinding and stamping until there was nothing left but a mold-colored smear in the worn carpet. Panting, he collapsed onto the bed, his hands pressed to his forehead.

"Well, that was fun," Grace said, slightly winded herself. "But we still don't know where Nelson is."

"Yes, we do." A.J. pointed to the ceiling.

She raised her eyes, and her stomach dropped. The emergency hatch above the bed was closed, but the black smears at the edges were unmistakable. It looked as if it had been pushed open by someone with two bloody, handless stumps.

She picked up the last unused blade and raced out the door.

"Stay here," she called back to her woozy companion. "I'll find him."

Chapter Eight

The mall was even more desolate than usual, due in part to the mountainous briar patch choking the East Hallway, a testament to the previous night's trial. It had been half a day since they had killed the witch, but the brambles she'd created remained, now covered in mottled gray and black spots and leeching a wet, dirty-shower smell into the closed space. Cari quickened her pace as she passed through the thicket toward the low arch that led into the rotunda. Harmless or not, they still stank.

She wandered from one end of the mall to the other, exploring far-off nooks and crannies she hadn't seen in forever. Then again, "forever" was a kind of relative. Had it only been ten days since she and Rex had sat in the movie theater lobby, scarfing down nachos and playing *Splatterfield 3*? Ten days since her biggest problem was being laid off and knowing she'd have to spend all her time at home with her mom? She nearly choked on the lump that thought brought to her throat. Her mother was a mean drunk with terrible taste in men, and that was putting it nicely.

But she didn't deserve this.

Cari sat down on the edge of the Atlas fountain. The soft splash of water trickling down his shoulders and into the basin did nothing to ease her despair. Instead, it brought back memories. Or rather, part of a memory. The only good one she had of her mom. Sunshine and lapping water. The smell of charcoal and grilling meat. Her mother with her hands around Cari's wrists, spinning faster and faster until Cari's feet left the ground. She closed her eyes and smiled. For a few seconds, it felt like she was flying.

She wished she could go back in time and take back all the terrible thoughts. She wished she had never pleaded with God or fate or whatever to help her escape. She wished…

She wished she'd just gone home that night with the beer and the cigarettes, and never started any of this at all.

The water splashed louder, bringing her back to the ground and reality. Pain wrapped itself around her chest and the tears flowed hot enough to sting and burn.

"It's not fair," she screamed at the pink glass dome above her. "It's not fucking *fair!*"

"What's not fair?"

"Shit!" She recoiled and almost fell backward, grabbing the lip of the bench in time to stop herself from falling into the fountain. She swiped her hands over her eyes as Cooper emerged from the shadows below the bridge. "You shouldn't sneak up on people like that!"

"Sorry," he said, his hands stuffed in the pockets of his slacks. "I only wanted to…are you okay?"

"I'm fine!" she snapped. "What are you even doing here anyway? I thought you were still on restricted duty."

He scowled. "That's not necessary. I don't know why I have to keep repeating that, seeing how I saved the day last night."

Cari arched an eyebrow. "As I recall, you weren't the only one who did some day-saving, thank you very much."

"Point taken. Anyway, I'm not really here. I'm trying to find Grace. She's not at home and she's not answering her cell phone. Do you know if she's around?"

Cari's stomach clenched. To answer that question meant telling him about her mother, and Nelson, and what she herself had done, or almost did. It would make him worry—or worse, it would make him sympathize. She already had one guy trying desperately to make everything normal. She didn't need another one.

But Grace isn't answering her phone.

Given what Cari knew that Cooper didn't, she had even more reason to find that concerning.

"She's at my house. Four Winds Trailer Park. Number Three."

His frown intensified. "Oh?"

She sensed the inherent question in the word but held steadfast to her silence.

"Okay, then," he said at last. "I guess I'll head over there. Thanks."

"Sure." She hesitated for a moment. "Although...you might want to take your gun."

His gaze darkened as his eyebrows drew together. This time, the question would not remain unspoken. "Cari, what the hell is going on?"

"It's a long story." She lowered her eyes to the ground as she dragged herself to her feet. "Come on,

I'll walk you downstairs."

She accompanied Cooper as far as the hallway at the bottom of the stairs, getting out as much of the story as she could before she left him standing in front of his locker with a dumbfounded look on his face. As she approached the sofa, she heard whispers coming from his direction. She shot a look behind her and scowled as John, having emerged from his ICU ivory tower, spoke to Cooper in a subdued tone.

Of course, she thought, balling her fingers around the cuffs of her sweatshirt. Why not? Cooper was an adult. John *would* share information with *him*. But her? *Noooo*. She was just a stupid kid. She couldn't possibly be trusted to know the truth about her own family.

She fumed until she reached the couch. The 8-bit jubilance of the video game score felt like a dozen tiny drills in her skull. With Rex's attention consumed by the faux melee, Cari slipped out of the common area and down the hall to the bunk room. Eight bunk beds ran along the perimeter of the forest green windowless box, with six single cots filling the space in the middle.

She flopped into the nearest low bunk, turned her back to the room, and wished desperately for sleep. Nightly rest was no longer a necessity—one of the perks of her new role in life, apparently—and on the occasions she'd tried it anyway, all she'd managed was a browned-out half-slumber that left her feeling groggy and a little hungover. But she would gladly take dreamless fog over the out-and-out nightmare that reality had become. Breathing deep, her eyelids heavy, she neared the edge of that semi-sweet escape when the rapid shuffle of approaching footsteps drove her conscious once again.

"Cari? Can I speak to you for a moment?"

John's overly downy voice made her ears itch. She kicked the wall, then rolled up to sit. "What do *you* want?"

He dropped down on the bed across from her and clasped his hands between his knees. He looked so composed, his glasses polished and clean, every one of his gray hairs perfectly arranged. It made her furious. This man said he was doing everything he could to save her mother, and yet he looked like he was ready for a board meeting.

"I'll be straight with you," he said. "Your mother has been fully infected with the conversion agent. Now, normally, after this much time has passed, we would be seeing a rapid decline in mental and physical stability that would necessitate a swift and merciful dispatch. However, the trajectory of your mother's conversion is not following that path. Instead, it seems to be more aligned with Holly's path. Slower, and not as all-consuming. Which means she will likely remain viable for significantly longer."

Cari's nails drove into her palms as snippets of a previous conversation floated through her mind. She knew what was coming. Still, she really, *really* hoped she was wrong.

"The bottom line is, though I can't cure her, there might still be hope. The best course now is to keep her confined and under observation and see how things progress from here."

Cari looked down at her hands. Her palms were filled with tiny red half-moons. "Like Holly."

"Precisely," John said. "In a way, it's fortunate that we had her here first. Holly's presence has allowed me to test numerous potential antidotes already. Now that there's two of them, I'm confident we will be able to recover them both eventually."

"How long?" she whispered.

"I beg your pardon?"

"You heard me. How. Long. How long before you'll have an antidote?"

"Cari, this is unexplored territory. There's no way to predict—"

Her head snapped up. "So, let me make sure I understand. You want to lock my mother in a cell and use her as a guinea pig until whenever, while you look for a cure that might not exist. Right?"

He frowned, his eyes widening slightly with surprise. "I'm sorry I can't give you a better timeline, but...Cari, this is good news. She could *survive* this." He reached for her hands. "I thought you would be happy."

"*Happy?*" Her body drained of all feeling as she leapt to her feet. Though she wasn't quite tall enough to tower over him, seeing him shrink back filled her with spiteful joy. "Bullshit. I know what's really going on. You *told* me you wanted to use Holly to try to communicate with these monsters. Now, you think you'll double your chances of catching one of them at home if you have two. You want to turn my mother into a two-way radio, and that's supposed to make me *happy*? Fuck you!"

She tore out of the room—or rather, her body tore out. Her thoughts floated a few feet behind. Her vision blurred as if she were riding in a rocket ship, and when it cleared, she stood outside the barred door to her mother's cell. Four leather straps fastened Libby to the cot. An IV stuck out of her arm connected to a bag filled with a chartreuse liquid that reminded Cari of antifreeze.

"Cari, wait! Can we please discuss this rationally?"

John's voice snaked up behind her, doubling her rage. She wanted to punch him right in the mouth. Instead, she dropped a hand to her holster.

"Don't come any closer!" she screamed, whipping toward John, ax wound up and ready to throw.

"Okay!" He ground to a halt, hands up at chin level. "I'll stay right here, I promise."

"Good." She tilted her head toward the bars. "Let me see her."

"That's not going to help."

"You could fix her if you wanted to!" Cari screamed, her voice shaking. Behind John, she saw a flash of black hair as Rex peeked around the corner, spotted the ax, and ducked away.

"I swear, I've done everything I can do for her," John whispered. "Maybe I didn't do a good job of explaining it before. Will you please let me try—"

"There's nothing else to say." She pulled her arm back further. "I've asked to see her a hundred times. I'm not asking anymore. Let me see her *right fucking now*!"

"Dude, read the room!" Rex shouted at John from his cover spot. "In case you didn't notice, you do *not* have the high ground here."

"Thank you, Mr. Ranganathan." John raised his stony eyes to the ceiling. "Mr. Mackie, please open Holding Cell Two."

"You sure, Boss?" Simon's wary voice fluttered down from the overhead speaker.

He met Cari's eyes. The pity in his face made her even more furious. "I'm sure. Open it."

The pause that followed ended in a heavy metal *chunk!* as the locks released. Her attention still on John, Cari slipped inside and hauled the door shut behind her.

"If you're not going to help her," she spat at him, "then I'll figure it out myself."

Chapter Nine

Grace flew off the stoop and dashed toward the back of the trailer. The sun had dipped behind the clouds huddling around the peaks of the western mountains, giving her at least some hope of cover. Good thing too—between her disheveled appearance and the knife, people might think she was trying to kill someone.

Well, some *human*, anyway.

A trail of oily sludge stained the back wall of the house. *That must be where he jumped down.* She scanned the ground and found more blood splashed over the packed dirt, splotchy lily pads that led to the woods. She squinted into the leafy murk, perplexed. Nelson lived in the park. He knew there was nothing beyond the trees except mountains and desert. Was he really trying to run for the wilderness? *Now?* She didn't know much about regeneration, but something as physiologically complex as a hand…that would probably take a while. And he was missing both. With no way to defend himself, he'd be easy pickings for a wolf or a bear. If something like that decided to make a meal of Nelson's corrupt, infectious flesh...what the hell kind of monster would they be dealing with then?

She didn't want to find out.

Holding the knife like a sword, she pushed forward, batting away the dense, slender branches as she followed the black streaks marring the underbrush. They got thinner the further she went, with more clean landscape between sightings. Still, she pressed on, scanning the woods for broken twigs, trodden leaves, and any other signs of disruption. She couldn't let Nelson infect anything else. Or worse, what if he somehow survived the rugged terrain and found a new town? He had fooled everyone in Halcyon for years. He could do it again, only this time there would be no one to stop him.

Leaves and branches lashed her cheeks as she broke into a jog. She had to find him. She had to end him. She had...

...lost the trail?

Her heart sank and her eyes searched the ground. How long had the splotches been missing? A few minutes? The last one she remembered had been barely more than a dribble, but maybe if she retraced her steps—

A thick appendage wrapped itself around her waist. Her hands flew up to try and defend herself, but it was too late—it pinned her arms to her side, jostling the knife from her grip as it did so.

"Fuck!" she gasped, her heart racing as a second sinewy thing hooked itself under her chin and squeezed her throat.

"I knew you'd come." The voice slithered into her left ear. "And just in time for group."

Her brain did a somersault. The prayer group. The army. He was doing the conversion tonight. That must have been why he'd turned Libby first, so he'd have some help. But he was a resourceful son of a bitch. No reason to think he couldn't do it alone.

She snapped her neck to the left, hoping to connect with his jaw, or maybe teeth.

He must have felt her muscles tense because he pulled back at the last moment, and she hit nothing but air.

"Now, now," he murmured, tightening his grip, "there's no need to be nervous. They're going to love you. Who doesn't love *snacks*?"

Grace opened her mouth to scream. With the speed of a cobra, his arm unfurled from her neck and coiled over her jaw instead. Cold, swollen flesh lodged itself between her lips, smothering her cries before they happened. Her tongue recoiled as the rancid stench of his skin invaded her nose. In the corner of her vision, three pill-sized white protuberances emerged from the tattered stump where he'd ripped his own hand off. Except for the translucent sliver of fingernail on the tip of each one, they reminded her of maggots trying to wriggle free of a corpse.

He yanked her backward. She raged against his hold the entire way to the tree line, snapping her neck and kicking her legs, all to no avail. She sucked air through her nose to stave off the panic as her thoughts turned desperate. Would A.J. come for her? He'd seemed pretty punch drunk when she'd left him. If not that, then…someone else?

But who would that be?

The forest around her began to glow, reflecting a light source she couldn't see. Her heartrate spiked. They were nearly at the park. Soon they'd be at his house, with his disciples. And Leann. Maybe even his two girls. If he made it back, they were *all* screwed.

She grazed her teeth over the flesh lodged in her mouth. It felt delicate and mushy, like an overripe strawberry. It wouldn't take much, and she knew he would feel the pain. Sure, it would mean horrible things for *her*. Infection, eventually death, but also escape. And the chance to save a hell of a lot more people.

She looked at the ground. The large black smears were barely discernible from the rest of the darkness. Another step, and they emerged from the woods.

Now or never.

She opened her jaw as wide as she could, aimed for the fleshiest part of his arm, and steeled her gag reflex as she prepared to bite.

An explosion rocketed past her head and knocked them both off their feet. Nelson's grip loosened as he fell to his knees. She threw herself out of his reach, her vision blurry and her skull ringing like the inside of a belfry.

"What the *hell?*" Nelson spluttered. His disoriented gaze wandered from the ground to the woods, and then to her. "You…"

She screamed as the second blast ripped through Nelson's chest. Darkness sprayed the tree trunks and saplings in front of him.

"Son of a bitch," he managed to slur around the glut of blood in his mouth before pitching forward into the dirt.

Grace stared at the perforated body, watching for movement, and waiting for the ringing in her head to subside. When it finally did, she lifted her eyes toward the trailer park, the smoking barrel, and the man standing behind it.

"You good?" Cooper asked, his voice tight as he lowered the shotgun to his side.

Her body trembled with joy and relief and anger. He was here. He was injured. He should have been here helping from the beginning. He should be at home recovering. He had saved her life. She wanted to hug him—and wring his neck a little. But most of all she wanted to tell him that she was *never* going to agree to do anything like this again unless he was along for the ride.

"Grace?"

She wiped an inky smear from her cheek and pointed at his gun. "I don't care what A.J. says. Best. Weapon. Ever."

"What's all that racket?" In the trailer next to Cari's, a shadowy outline of a man appeared in the window, hunkered down as if trying to see through the darkness.

"Sorry 'bout that!" Cooper shouted back. "Damn raccoons were getting into the trash cans again. Nothing to worry about."

The figure shook his head, mumbled something about "black eyed demons," and disappeared from view.

"Nice cover." Grace hauled herself to her feet and grabbed Nelson by his partially regenerated stumps. "Let's get this bastard inside before he wakes up."

"He took an AA-12 blast through the chest. He's *done*." Cooper narrowed his eyes at her. "Isn't he?"

"Not even a little."

"Ah." He smirked and shook his head. "You see? This is what happens when I take a day off."

***

A.J. greeted them at the door. They scuttled into the trailer with Nelson's undead weight sagging between them like a sack of potatoes.

"There." A.J. pointed at the bed. Additional lengths of rope lay across the mattress, along with a pile of wrinkled pants and shirts.

"I see you've been busy," Grace grunted as she hefted Nelson on the bouncy surface.

A.J. picked up one of the thick twine cords, his face stony. "We're not taking any chances this time."

He wrapped Nelson from neck to ankles in the clothing until he looked like the world's most disgusting burrito before strapping him down. He had nearly finished when Nelson flopped his head to the side and slid one eyelid open.

"Where am I?" he moaned.

"Purgatory, you dick," Grace shot back. "Now shut your mouth and let the grownups talk."

A.J. gagged him with the dishrag and the three of them retreated to the main room.

"Now," Cooper said softly, keeping one eye on Nelson through the cracked door, "can someone please tell me what the fuck is going on?"

"If we're going to go through the whole thing, we might as well tell everyone." Grace retrieved her phone and dialed John's cell.

"Speaking of explaining things," she asked Cooper over the speakerphone ringing, "what the hell are you doing here anyway?"

"Right!" He tore his vigilant gaze away from Nelson. "I almost forgot. Lola called me. She's been trying to reach you all day. Which is funny, since I don't seem to recall you two ever even meeting each other."

"Oh?" she asked, trying to sound casual. Not easy, seeing as her tongue had gone as dry as a dune. "Yeah, we've met. But I haven't seen her in a few years now. Did she tell you what she wanted to talk to me about?"

"No, and I didn't think it was my place to ask. But it sounded important, and she's not the type of person who blows things out of proportion."

Grace nodded as sepia-colored snapshot of her last interaction with Lola flickered at the edge of her consciousness, fuzzy at first, but rapidly becoming clearer. She gripped the phone tighter and snuffed out the memory before it could fully manifest. That was not something she needed to relive. Especially not today.

Cooper's gaze fell across her, heavy with suspicion. She shrugged, as if her dread was nothing more than absent-minded reminiscing. "I'll call her after we finish up with…um, has it been ringing this whole time?"

They stared at the small brick of blue light in her hand. John never let it ring this long. A sinkhole formed in her gut.

Something wasn't right.

"Do we have anyone else's number?"

"Yeah." Cooper pulled out his cell and tapped the screen. "I think I've got Rex in here somewhere."

This time, it only rang twice.

"Whoever this is, I can't talk right now."

"Don't hang up!" Grace shouted. Her nerves, soothed by the fact he had answered, tensed back up as soon as she tagged the panic in his voice. "It's us. Me and A.J. and Cooper. What's going on?"

"I…I don't really know what's happening, but we've got a situation here. With Cari. And her mom."

Muffled shouting muddled the background of the call. She couldn't decipher the words, but she knew the voice as John's.

And he sounded terrified.

"Put us on speaker," Grace instructed, making her voice as stern and solid as she could. "If you can't explain it, then at least we can hear for ourselves."

Chapter Ten

Libby lay on the bed, as fragile and immobile as a bundle of twigs. Despite her eagerness and the adrenaline coursing down her limbs, Cari forced herself to move slowly, the way she had when her mother was in the middle of a drunken tear. She approached with soft, deliberate steps, careful not to jump or jerk. The closer she got to her mother's bedside, the more her stomach revved with uncertainty. She meant it when she said she wanted to help. But what the hell did help even *look* like?

A soft moan slipped from between Libby's pale lips, halting Cari next to her mother's elbow. She examined the vicious IV sinking into the waxy, yellowing flesh.

What can I do? What...

Her eyes slid from the bed to the ax in her hand.

It had worked for Rex. Maybe it would work here.

She adjusted her grip to hold the ax by the back of its metal head and brought the corner of the blade down to the inside of her mother's fish-belly forearm, right below the tape holding the needle in place.

"It's not going to work."

She flicked her eyes toward the bars. John stood on the other side, hands in his pockets, while Rex lurked behind him. Her grip tightened. She wasn't stupid. He could come in if he wanted to. One word to Simon and that cage door would slide right open. Instead, he stood there, watching her, his face all scrunched up in pity.

Useless.

Scowling in defiance, she turned back to her mother and lowered the blade. A trickle of black-and-green liquid bloomed from the cut. Libby whimpered, her closed eyes screwing up in pain. Cari pressed harder, drawing the blade further down her arm. Once the cut reached six inches in length she withdrew, watching the wound bleed. And bleed.

And bleed.

Her eyeballs throbbed as her heart spun up into a panic. Libby's lips and eyelids had turned the color of frosted blueberries, and still the blood remained the color of nightshade.

She shook her head in refusal. It had to turn. It had to.

Maybe if she did the other arm…

Stealth no longer a priority, she tore around the head of the bed and pressed her blade to Libby's right arm.

"Cari, please. You don't want to do this."

She paused, ax hovering an inch from flesh. The heat of her anger surged through her fingers, compelling her to let the blade bite.

"Why not?" she spat back at John.

"Because it will kill her," he said. "The infection burrows too far below the surface. You could bleed her dry and it wouldn't help."

"Did you try it?" Her voice shook almost as much as her hand.

"We've tried it before. Many times, and every one of them—"

"I'm not talking about other people!" Cari shrieked, her voice nearly breaking. "Did you try it on *her?*"

He sighed. "No, I did not try it on her."

"Then how do you know it won't work?"

"Because…" He wiped a hand over his face as if that could start things fresh. "If you let her live, we might be able to cure her eventually. If you kill her now, then that's it. You'll lose her forever."

She shook her head. The blade in her hand zigged, nicking the soft skin. A single drop of blood appeared, as black as a starless night. "I've already lost her."

"She's right, John."

Cari's body stiffened as a female voice, slightly Southern and honey-sweet, wandered into range.

John shot a furious glare in the direction of Cell One. "*You* stay out of this."

"Who is that?" Cari shouted. "Is that Holly?"

"Technically?" Rex leaned back to see around the dividing wall. "Doesn't sound like any voice I've ever heard her use though."

"It's Mary."

She jumped at Cooper's buzzy, disembodied words. *Where the hell was that coming from?* Then she spotted the phone in Rex's hand. "Who?" she demanded.

"Mary Fludd. The Reverend's wife."

"That's right," the voice called Mary confirmed, its warmth and kindness making Cari shiver. "And I swear, I come as a friend. I'm sorry, little one, but your mother has one foot across the threshold and the other isn't far behind. You can't stop her from going, and neither can the good doctor over there. But there is a way you can see her one last time. I can tell you how."

"Stay out of this!" John shouted. He whipped his eyes toward Cari. "Don't listen to her. You know she can't be trusted."

"She needs something familiar," Mary continued "Something that appeals to her senses. Her favorite perfume, a special song. Something that reminds her what it was like to be human. *Her* version of human."

Cari's head ached, and every muscle in her body screamed with exhaustion. The settlers were monsters. How could she trust this one?

Because if I don't, then I might as well slit my mother's throat right now.

She opened her eyes and scanned the cell. Not much there. The bed, her mom, herself, and a small table crammed with pills, tonics, and sterilization tools.

Including rubbing alcohol.

The ax clattered on the concrete floor as Cari grabbed the bottle and tore off the cap. The astringent scent stung her nose. Holding her breath, she poured the contents into her mother's open mouth. Libby's eyes flew open as she wretched against the onslaught.

"No!" John shouted. "Mr. Mackie, the door!"

The metal gears groaned alive behind her. Cari ignored them. Instead, she grasped her mother by the forehead and jaw and clamped her mouth shut. Libby bucked and squealed, shooting some of the burning liquid out of her closed lips and nostrils. Still, Cari held on, and didn't let go until John grabbed her shoulders and yanked her away.

"Have you lost your mind?" He spun her around to face him. "You know those things have their own agenda. You might have created some kind of super solider, or a spawning point for an army of creatures, or—"

"Cari?"

Her skin turned to ice. She knew that voice, yet it had become so much softer and more delicate it seemed like something out of dream.

Or a memory.

Struggling against John's grip, she craned her neck to look behind her. From the bed blinked the blue eyes of Libby Hembert, confused but as clear as sapphires. "Cari...what...what's going on?"

Her legs became liquid, and she went limp. Her jaw flapped numbly as she struggled to form words. At last, she managed to get out the one that mattered. "Mom?"

John's fingers dug into her arms. "I don't believe it," he sighed, but the bewilderment in his voice suggested otherwise. "It must be a...trick, or something."

Cari wriggled out of his hands and dove for her mother's bedside.

"Mom, I'm here," she said, entwining her mother's slick, black-stained fingers with her own. John made no move to stop her, but she could feel his presence hovering at her side.

"Cari..." Libby tried to sit up, but the restraints wouldn't allow her to do much more than lift her head. "Why can't I move?"

"Because...you're sick, Mom. Really sick. It's for all of our protection. Yours and ours."

"Sick? But I don't..." Her eyes widened with horrified clarity. "It was Nelson, wasn't it?"

Cari bit her lip and nodded.

"Jesus." Libby fell back and squeezed her eyes shut. "I remember. His wife and girls had gone to visit her mother, and he came over, like he always did when they went to Grandma's. But this time he was acting funny. He made me drink. Even more than normal, until I couldn't stand, and then his face went all rubbery and…and his eyes…" She whimpered and peered up at her daughter. "I don't have much time, do I?"

The words crashed into Cari like a wrecking ball. She tried to answer, but the words stuck in her throat. All she could do was bow her head and clasp her mother's hand even tighter.

Libby exhaled sharply. The tears in her eyes broke free, streaming down her temples to pool next to her ears. "I'm sorry, sweetie. I'm so sorry for bringing that man into our lives, and for all my mistakes and for…all of it."

Cari nodded as guilt and anger waged burning war inside her heart. She had so many things she wanted to say (or cry, or scream), but the pain had stolen the moisture from her tongue. If she tried to speak, she feared she would crumble to dust.

Libby cocked her head toward John. "Who are you?"

He cleared his throat. "Doctor John Virgil, ma'am. I'm her…supervisor."

"Good." Libby sat up as high as she could. "You look after my girl, you understand? You do what I can't…what I never could."

John swallowed hard. "I will, ma'am. I promise."

Libby nodded, satisfied. Her head fell back once more, and she returned her attention to Cari. Despite the restraints and Cari's own iron grip, she could feel her mother's fingers tighten around her own. "My little girl. Everything is going to be okay now. You're so much stronger and smarter than I ever was, even at my best. You're going to do great things, I know it. Wherever I go next, I hope I'll be able to see you do them."

Her eyes fluttered, and she groaned in pain. "But I don't think that's a wish I will be getting."

Her grip turned to jelly.

Cari's heart pounded. "Mom?"

Libby didn't answer. She shook her mother's hand. It was as limp and cold as raw chicken. "No," she spluttered. "Not yet. Mom! Can you hear me?"

Libby's chest rose. Cari's breath caught in her throat as her mother let go with one long, rasping breath.

"I love you."

In the sixteen years she'd spent on the planet, Cari couldn't remember her mother ever saying that to her before. Now she would never, ever forget it.

"I love you too."

She released her mom and sank to her knees. Sobs thrashed her like a tree in a storm. Her breath grew shallow as she tried to contain the sloshing and quaking in her stomach. For as long as she could recall, she had always *felt* like she was alone in the world. But that was nothing compared to the full-body assault of *knowing* she was.

I'm an orphan. She wrapped her arms around herself and pressed her forehead to the cold, rough concrete as brown shadows danced in front of her tunneling vision. *What's going to happen to me now?*

The last thing she remembered was the warm strength of John's arms, gathering her up and lifting her into…

Nothing.

Chapter Eleven

Cooper hit the Mute button and cleared his throat. "Well, that was…"

"Difficult," Grace supplied, swiping at the tears that had collected on her eyelashes. On the other side of the trailer A.J. stood facing away from them, one hand braced on his hip and the other raised to his down-turned face. If he heard them speaking, he didn't acknowledge it.

"Yes." Cooper nodded. "It was difficult. But…"

"But we still have work to do." Grace pivoted toward the bed. A man, bound and half-mutilated, but improving by the second. A woman, dead, or close enough. Add them together and what did they have?

One giant fucking mess.

She pressed a hand to her forehead. "How the hell are we ever going to clean up this one?"

"Good question," Cooper mused, rubbing his chin. "We can't keep him alive, that's for sure. He's too dangerous, especially with the regeneration."

"Right, but we can't make him disappear either. He was only gone a few hours before his wife came looking for him. She didn't strike me as the type who would let a man run out on her without having something to say about it. And as far as leaving his body in a ditch..." She gestured widely at his half-formed hands and the soaked, caved-in dark spot on his chest. "One look at him and even the Dudley Do-Nothings at Halcyon PD will know something's up. Not to mention that, if we don't kill him perfectly, he'll get right back up again."

He frowned. "And by 'perfectly,' you mean...?"

She paused, searching for the best words to describe what she was picturing before answering.

"Bits and pieces. No more, no less."

"That's what I thought." He looked from Nelson to the stove, then back again, his eyes growing both resolute and apprehensive.

"I may have an idea," he said at last. "One that should account for everything."

Grace arched her eyebrow. "Sounds great. What's the catch?"

He tilted his head sheepishly and told them.

"Jesus," A.J. muttered, wiping his face with both hands.

She sneered at Cooper in disgust. "I take it back. It's not great. It's the worst idea I've ever heard."

"I'm not arguing that," Cooper said, his eyes on the floor. "But unless either of you have a better one..."

She didn't, and they both knew it. Even so, she pretended to consider it for a full minute out of spite.

"Fine," she relented.

"Okay." Cooper pressed Unmute. "Rex, you still there?"

A startled rustle followed. *"10-4, buddy. I'm still here."*

"Good. Can you take us off speaker?"

"Sure." He disappeared for a second before returning, this time louder and much less tinny. *"Go ahead."*

"I think we've got a plan to deal with Nelson. You'll need to meet us at the trailer."

"Really?" Rex sounded stunned. *"You're tapping me in. Me?"*

Cooper smiled. "Yes, man. I'm tapping you in."

"Well, it's about time! I'll grab my stuff and be right there."

"Hold on a second, Dynamite. There's one more thing." He took a deep breath. "Can you put Cari on the phone? We need to, ah, run something by her first."

"Um, I don't know if that's such a good idea. She's, you know…pretty out of it."

"I know, but this is really important. We can't do anything without her sign-off."

Silence took the line as Rex thought it over. *"Okay. But if anything you say freaks her out, I'm cutting you off. Capisce?"*

"Capisce."

Grace pinned her gaze to the phone. She didn't want Cooper to see how Rex's loyalty made her smile. More silence followed, then some incoherent mumbling, and finally Cari's voice.

"Yeah…?"

Grace's heart broke at how fragile the word sounded.

"Hey, Cari." Cooper's cheeks had turned red with the shame of what he was about to say, but he pressed forward. "Listen, I know you've been through a lot today, and I don't even want to bring this up, but…we've still got to take care of Nelson. There's a way to do it, but…"

Heavy thumps drew Grace's attention as A.J. retreated away from the conversation toward the bathroom, unable to listen. She couldn't say she blamed him.

"...awful thing to ask, but it's our only option." Cooper inhaled deeply. His cheeks had turned the color of tomato sauce, as if he hadn't taken a breath since he started talking.

The pause on the other end of the line was so full and complete Grace briefly wondered if she had hung up on them, or possibly passed out from the shock.

"You're sure it's the only way?" Cari ventured.

Cooper smiled sadly. "It's the only way to guarantee this all ends tonight."

"And Nelson will be dead?"

"Yes, honey," Grace said, her voice as sweet and smooth as frosting. "He's gonna be real dead."

Another long silence. When her voice returned, it sounded about as fragile as braided steel.

"Do it."

Grace and Cooper prepped the bedroom as best they could while A.J. ran to town for extra supplies. The three of them had almost finished situating things by the time John pulled up in Libby's half-wrecked Prelude. The muscles between Grace's shoulders loosened as she watched Rex climb out of the passenger's side, messenger bag slung across his shoulder. She never would have thought the sight of that goofy kid would come as such a massive relief.

Then he tipped the seat forward, and Cari crawled out from the backseat.

"Goddammit," Grace snarled as her muscles seized up again. She stormed out the door and grabbed Rex by the sleeve.

"What were you thinking?" she demanded once she'd dragged him out of Cari's earshot. "Hasn't she been through enough without seeing this?"

The defensive fury in his glare made her delay further ranting.

"She'll never be able to come back here," he said, throwing her hand off him. "I *thought* she deserved the chance to grab some stuff. Little things, you know, like her phone charger, and toothbrush, and *everything she owns in the world.*"

Grace took a step back, stunned and ashamed. She'd been so focused on the plan it had completely slipped her mind that, at least for the next few minutes, this was someone's home.

"You're right. I'm sorry. Just...give me one second."

She ducked her head inside to make sure the bedroom door was closed, then motioned for Rex. He let Cari lead the way up the stoop and into the trailer.

"Hey," Grace said, the syllable ragged and uneasy at the sight of Cari's lopsided ponytail, folded-over slouch and dull, sunken eyes. "I'm, uh…"

She wasn't sure how to finish the sentence. Regardless, Cari shrugged and bobbled her head in a vague gesture of acceptance.

Rex slipped a hand over her shoulder and squeezed. "Which way?"

She tipped her head to her left and trudged down the narrow center hallway toward the small door in the back. When she flipped on the light, Grace spotted the outline of a twin bed jammed in a crawlspace so tight that Rex could barely close the door. It didn't look big enough to house a hamster, let alone a teenager.

With the kids otherwise occupied, she tapped her knuckles on the bedroom door. It opened a crack, revealing a single blue eye.

"What's the password?"

"Move, Cooper."

"Wow, first try." The door swung open the rest of the way.

She slipped inside and closed it behind her. "Where are we?"

A.J. wrapped a hand over the wrought iron headboard and gestured toward the room with the other. "Last looks."

She took the visual tour. The semi-conscious Nelson was once again hooked to the headboard with the handcuffs, the restraints reinforced with six sets of snagged pantyhose. Thick ropes looped over the mattress, strapping him down so tight that the skin below the rough twine had already started to chafe. The sundry items from the dresser and vanity had been knocked onto the floor to make room for the dozens of candles A.J. had brought from town, supplementing the four or five half-melted ones already oozing across the cheap furniture. The candles on the right side of the room glowed like two dozen tiny suns. The ones on the left were dark.

"Not bad," she said.

A soft rap at the door made her turn. "We're done." Rex's strained voice struggled to make its way into the room. "I'm taking her outside. Let me know when you want me to...uh, when you're ready."

"Thanks," she mumbled back. It pained her to hear him sound so sad. "A.J., why don't you drive her back to Edensgate. She doesn't need to be here for the rest."

A.J. tipped a solemn finger to his forehead.

"I'll walk you out," Cooper said. "John's probably gonna need some help." He handed the box of matches to Grace. "Will you be okay by yourself?"

She took the box and nodded. Only when the door had closed behind the two men, and she stood alone in the room did she allow her shoulders to sag. She hated this day. She hated everything that had happened so far and everything that was about to happen. She hated this plan, and that Cooper had been the one to think of it, and that she was too stupid to come up with a better one.

But even if she could stop this train now, she wouldn't. It was the best solution. And she hated *that* too.

She struck a match and kissed the flame to the first unlit wick. Some days, fighting an inter-dimensional war on evil could be a real bitch.

A low, insidious rumble brought a tremor to her hand. She glanced over her shoulder at the bed. Nelson gazed up at her, eyes shining, and lips stretched in a tight smile. When he caught her looking, the rumble became a wet chuckle.

"Laugh while you can," she spat. "Won't be long now."

"Killing me won't change anything," he said around his laughter. "The Prophet approaches. He will open the Primal Seal with or without me."

"Without. If it makes no difference, let's go with that."

He dropped his head back onto the mattress, his deep laughter steady and thoroughly unsettling. She turned back to the wax army on the dresser.

"Aren't you going to ask me what's so funny?"

"Nope." Her hand swept from wick to wick, eager to get this over with.

"It's funny because, deep down, you know what I'm saying is the truth. You see what's really going on in this town. The abdication of responsibility. The selfishness, and the cruelty. You can rip yourself to pieces fighting the enemy at the gate, but the castle is already rotting from the inside. And there's not a thing you can do about that."

She wanted to punch him in his cavernous chest wound. Instead, she lit another match. "You're so right. Life is hard and people suck. I should stand aside and let the hordes of hell take over."

"You can call it that if you want to. Or you can call it what it is: a new start. An era without the cowardice, hatred and greed that has been humanity's legacy on this planet."

The droplet of flame crept down the matchstick, coming dangerously close to her fingertips. She shook it out, the vigorous movement a perfect disguise for her shaking limbs, and turned around to look at him one last time.

"I don't believe you."

"You don't have to." He closed his eyes. His smile no longer looked menacing, but serene. "You'll see it for yourself. Someday."

She shivered. He didn't sound like a possessed maniac anymore. Instead, he sounded sad, and exhausted, like a reasonable human being that had seen too much.

Who couldn't relate to that?

The thought squirmed in her brain like a snake, its fangs exposed and ready to bite. She shook her head, trying to smash it against the inside of her skull. But more words wormed their way in.

You can't protect her. Her flesh is marked for us. She is ours.

Grace froze. *What the fuck does that mean?*

She ventured one last look at Nelson. His eyes rolled in their sockets as he bared his slick, drool-covered teeth. He craned his face toward the ceiling and crowed with laughter, savoring her distress. He was dying, but he was winning. She couldn't let that happen. She searched the room, the bed, the dresser…and there, in a shadowy corner near where A.J.'s arsenal had been, she spotted something interesting. Something A.J. must have missed when he was packing up.

She grabbed the syringe filled with venom and plunged it into Nelson's neck. Laughter morphed into a scream, which she stifled with the first thing she could find—a pair of lime green panties.

"I don't know what's gonna happen down the road," she whispered to his lolling eyeballs. "No one does. But here's something I do know: you're going to get what you deserve, and you're going to feel it. Every. Fucking. Second."

She ripped the needle from his flesh. The last thing she saw before turning her back on him was the geyser of black blood splashing across the mattress.

"Enjoy oblivion, asshole."

She slammed out the door. The night had gone frigid, and she paused to gulp down a couple mouthfuls of frosty air before descending from the stoop.

"All set?" Cooper asked as he and John approached the trailer, carrying a semi-conscious Libby suspended between them. A thick patch of medical tape covered her mouth, but it seemed unnecessary. In her current state, she looked about as threatening as a bag of cooked spaghetti. Behind them, Rex sulked next to the open trunk, fiddling with the strap of his bag, his eyes trained on a rock near his feet. She didn't see Cari or A.J. anywhere.

"Yeah," Grace murmured, her attention drawn to Libby. She wanted to say something to the woman. Apologize, or something, even though she didn't know what for. But Libby's eyes never opened more than halfway. "You've sedated her."

"Heavily," John said as he led the way up the steps. "She won't feel a thing."

Grace watched with a heavy heart as they took her into the house. Sedation was the right call.

Anything she would have said would've probably sounded dumb anyway.

She shuffled over to Rex. "You ready?"

"Yeah," he said sulkily. "I still don't like it though."

"Can't say I blame you. She's your girlfriend's mom, after all."

Rex threw up his hands. "For the last time, Cari is *not* my girlfriend. *GOD!*"

"First of all, *shhh!*" Grace scanned the area, making sure the mostly abandoned section of the park had stayed that way before continuing. "And second of all…are you absolutely sure about that?"

"Yes!" Rex shouted, then ducked at the sound of his own voice. "She's not…we're…yes, I'm sure."

"Fine. Whatever you say." She leaned back against the trunk next to him.

"Why, did she say something about me?"

Grace shook her head. Thank God she didn't have to be sixteen ever again.

Moments later, John and Cooper emerged from the house, Libby no longer draped between them.

"That's your cue, kid." Grace nudged Rex with her elbow. He sighed and peeled himself off the car.

Cooper stood guard next to the door when Rex went inside, weapon at the ready. Five minutes later Rex emerged, tucking something back under the flap of his messenger bag.

"Done."

"And it'll look like an accident?" Grace confirmed.

"Yeah. Enough to fool the geniuses at Halcyon PD, anyway." He smiled reluctantly. "It's actually pretty cool, how it works. All you gotta do is—"

"Let's hold off on the incendiary lessons, shall we?" Grace said. "You and Cooper can head back. John and I will stand watch to make sure nothing goes wrong."

"Or escapes," John supplemented.

"That too," she said. "Besides, we have a lot of catching up to do."

Grace crouched behind a thick tree trunk, waiting in silence as John processed the rundown she'd given him regarding the day's events. Across the clearing, the windows of the trailer pulsed with the soft orange glow of the candlelight. She could see no other movement, hear no other sound. Under the not-quite-full moon, the night was crystalline and deathly quiet.

"This isn't right."

She jumped at the sound of her own voice, thunderous in the pristine stillness. She hadn't expected to say it out loud so abruptly, though it had been on her mind ever since Cooper had come up with this horror show. Tying up Nelson's loose end would make sure no spotlights came their way. It wasn't perfect, but it *was* necessary. Still, it didn't change the fact that, in the course of twenty-four hours, a sixteen-year-old girl had lost everything. "We need to do something for her, John. Make sure she's taken care of."

Sticks and dried leaves crackled behind the tree to her left.

"She will be," John whispered, his voice a down quilt in the cold. "I promised her mother I'd look out for her, and that's exactly what I'm going to do."

Her eyes slipped closed in relief. Across the park, the light inside the trailer glowed even brighter.

"So, Nelson is an acolyte of the Reverend?" John mused.

"Seems that way," she affirmed.

"Did he infect anyone else?"

"I don't think so. He was planning to at his prayer circle tonight, but obviously he never made it."

"Thank God for that." John paused. "Still, it might be prudent to check on everyone in the group. And Nelson's family too."

"Copy that." She thought back to Simon's comment about the group's purported anonymity. "Might take a little time to track them all down, you know."

"That's fine, as long as it gets done." He drew in a long breath. She winced as the atmosphere between them tensed. *Here it comes...*

"Will there be more like him?"

And there it was. The question she'd been dreading all day.

"It's hard to know," she said as she fidgeted with her cell phone. "If this sort of conversion is limited to the Reverend's direct descendants, then probably not. Otherwise…"

She lowered her head, digging at a piece of bark with the tip of her fingernail to try to distract herself from what she had to say. "John, he walked around with a monster in his head for the better part of a decade. That's some messed up, *Manchurian Candidate*-type shit. If there's no genetic limitation, then all bets are off. Literally *anyone* in Halcyon could be infected, and we'd never know. And…if we assume there's even a *chance* that Nelson's little nursery rhyme is true…at least one more person must be."

"Indeed." John tipped his head toward her, his lens reflecting the moonlight. "Which means Edensgate is not our only responsibility anymore."

The statement dropped sixty pounds of lead square on her shoulders. Securing a building was one thing. How were the handful of them supposed to police a whole *town*? She opened her mouth to ask when she heard a hiss, then a pop. She turned back to the park as the trailer exploded in a firework of metal and glass. A wave of thunder slammed into her chest, stealing her breath and almost knocking her over.

"Christ," John muttered as the trailer shell dropped to the ground with a bang and settled into a steady, rapid blaze.

"Amen." Her shell-shocked fingers moved like uncooperative hot dogs over her phone, but at last she managed to press the right button.

"911, what is your emergency?" She could barely hear around the ringing in her ears.

"Oh my God!" she gasped. "A trailer just exploded at Four Winds! You need to get the fire department out here right now! Hurry!"

"Certainly ma'am. And can I please get your—?"

Grace hung up. "That ought to do it. We'll wait until they get here, see if anything tries to rip their faces off, then head out."

"Agreed."

They watched in silence for a moment as the tongues of fire stretched long, their light lapping at the navy sky.

"You know," Grace said, "if we are going to start patrolling the whole town, we're going to need more help."

John's chuckle was so dry it nearly disintegrated in midair.

"Don't we always?"

Chapter Twelve

Cari lost track of A.J. the moment he settled her on the couch. She sort of remembered him asking if she needed anything, and maybe something about going out on rotation. He hadn't seemed uncomfortable, or like he wanted to get away from her. Instead, he seemed to understand that hovering over her like a fussy mama pigeon would not be useful for either of them.

Finally, *someone* got it.

On the coffee table in front of her sat a cardboard box, its flaps origami-folded to keep them shut. The trip to the trailer floated through her mind in a barely retained fog of hastily grabbed items. Framed photos. Jewelry and makeup. A few treasured pieces of clothing. It had been one of those rare times when having almost no personal stuff had worked to her advantage. Even so, she didn't want to look inside the box. She didn't want to know what she'd left behind. What she would never see again.

Something moved behind her, slow and deliberate. Then came the voices. Cooper's first, followed by John's, both of them hushed and tenuous, as if the walls might collapse if they spoke any louder than a stage whisper. She registered a few scraps ("a week or two," "best option," "better solution later,"), and she definitely heard her name at least once. Everything else was a fat hum. Her brain had OD'd on emotion and information. She listened until the voice-noise faded, and silence reigned again. The loneliness pressed into her, choking and cutting at the same time, like a skeleton's hand around her heart.

"Cari?"

Startled, she looked up. Rex leaned over the back of the couch, peering down at her with weary, timid eyes.

"Hey," she said, the muscles of her face twitching into something that might have been a smile.

"Hey." He vaulted over the back of the couch and sat down next to her, rubbing his hands over his knees. "I, uh…huh. I guess I don't know what to say."

"That's okay," she sighed. "I don't feel much like talking anyway."

"Is there anything I *can* do to help?"

"Not really. Though…" She smiled weakly. "If it's not too much trouble…could you go back to playing your video game? I just want to watch."

"Really?" He stared at the controller on the table as if it were a week-old burrito. "I mean, don't you want to…cry, or yell, or…or maybe drink some tea? I'm not great at coffee, as you know, but I'm pretty good at tea."

At first, she could only stare at him. Then she exploded, all the anger and sorrow ripping through her numbness like a knife through paper. "Are you *kidding* me? You've done nothing all day except try to make everything seem normal, but as soon as I ask you to do exactly that, *now* you want to talk about feelings? Are you *serious*? Are…you…fucking…serious…"

She stopped yelling. Not because she wasn't still angry, but because she couldn't breathe. Stupid Rex, she thought, clenching her fists together as she gasped for air. Stupid Nelson. Stupid fucking world.

"It's okay." Rex slid his arm over her shoulders. "It's…going to be okay."

"No…it's…not," she wheezed, tears streaming down her cheeks. "My mom is *dead*. My house is *destroyed*. Everything is so completely *fucked up*." She kicked the cardboard box. "All I have left is this stupid pile of crap."

"And me." He wrapped his free hand around one of hers. "I'm still here."

She turned to face him. He tried to meet her gaze but seemed to be struggling to lift his eyes any higher than her chin. She frowned as she watched his lips twitch like a nervous rabbit. She'd seen him act strange plenty of times, but never like this. Never like—

Her heart started to race.

"Rex…you're not going to try to kiss me right now, are you?"

"What? No!" He recoiled as if her skin had sprouted thorns. "No, of course not. I would never do that. That would be so—"

She leaned forward and pressed her mouth to his.

He stiffened, probably as surprised as she was by her boldness. But the boy did protest too much, and this seemed like the quickest way to stop his flustering.

It worked. After a moment, she felt him relax. His lips parted, enveloping hers as he kissed her back. A spark of excitement glimmered through her. Now it was her turn to freeze.

She hadn't expected that.

Breaking the kiss, she leaned back a little so she could look at him. His eyes were still closed, and a goofy smile hung on his face.

"—so gross," he murmured dreamily.

She giggled. "Gross?"

"Yeah, super…disgusting…"

He reached for her again.

"Hey!"

The voice sent them shooting away from each other like opposing magnets. Heat flooded Cari's face as she turned to look over the back of the couch. Grace stood in the entryway outside the lockers, hands on her hips, and a mischievous grin lighting up her face. Next to her stood a tall man in the standard Virgil Security & Maintenance coveralls. He seemed slightly younger than Grace, with short black hair, dark brown skin, and twinkling brown eyes.

Or rather, his right eye twinkled. His left was obscured by a black leather patch.

"Sorry to bother you two," Grace said, her voice on the edge of a giggle. "We were just passing through this *very public area*, and I figured I'd take the opportunity to introduce you to Charlie. Charlie, this is Cari and Rex."

"Hi," Cari mumbled, waving her hand to draw attention from her presumably crimson cheeks. "Sorry, I…sorry. It's been a…rough night."

"Not a problem." He pointed to his left eye. "As you can see, I've had plenty of those myself. It's nice to meet you both."

"You too." A mosquito bite of a question itched the back of her mind. She frowned until it clicked. "Oh, Charlie! You're the guy that fell into the fountain last week, right?"

"Oh, yeah!" Rex's face lit up in recognition, and he pointed at Charlie with both index fingers. "Fountain Guy!"

Charlie turned to Grace. "Is that going to be a thing now?"

Grace shrugged. "We could call you Patchy instead. Up to you. Now come on, John wants to look you over before he signs off on your return." She arched an eyebrow at Rex as they headed for the med station. "Enjoy your totally platonic conversation."

Rex scowled after her, his face beet red.

"What was that all about?" Cari asked.

"Oh, you know." He flopped a dismissive hand toward the med station. "She keeps saying that we're…that you're my…anyway, don't worry about it. She's…crazy."

"Oh." Her heart crashed through the floor. "You're right. It would be crazy."

"No! I didn't mean it like that. I…uh…"

He trailed off. She couldn't believe it. The one time she needed him to say something, and he was at a loss for words. They both stared at the cushion's worth of space between them. She could feel the moment slipping away; it surprised her how desperate she was to cling to it. She'd never thought of Rex that way before. Okay, maybe not *never*. But never seriously. Never like…this. She cast around for something to say, something that would close the chasm that Grace's interruption had caused. Something…

"So, are you going to play your game?"

…besides that.

Rex smiled at his feet. "Sure, Mayhem. Whatever you want."

She wanted to believe she heard regret in his voice. Or was it relief? And how was she supposed to know the difference?

Ultimately, it didn't matter. Before she could dream up the perfect way to salvage the moment, Rex picked up the controller, turned away from her, and started the game.

Sunshine peeped above the trees, warming Cari's face through the truck's passenger window. To say it had been a slow night would have been an understatement bordering on felonious. At one point, when Grace had dropped by to check on them, she had mentioned that the night after a long moon was often slow. Cari kept her ears up anyway, waiting—and then wishing— for something to happen. But nothing did. She spent the whole night on the couch, watching Rex run through hundreds of 8-bit sparring matches and trying to pretend the silence between them was natural. By the time the doors opened in the morning, the elephant in the room had grown so massive they'd retreated to opposite sides of the couch to make room for it. He didn't even look up when Cooper asked to speak to her in private. He just turned his head slightly and saluted her knees.

Even now, miles away, the remembered awkwardness made her want to bury her head in her hands. As if enough of her life hadn't been literally blown to pieces today. Why did she have to go and kiss her best friend on top of it?

She pressed a hand to her forehead and tried not to think about it, concentrating on the scenery out her window instead. The town flowed by in a monotonous, gray-brown blur. On any other day she would be on the bus right now, rumbling down the country highway to the T-intersection outside the city limits, then onto the dirt road heading out to Four Winds. Instead, she was in this truck, her single box of possessions at her feet, turning right onto an asphalt one-way street that ran parallel to Halcyon's main drag. The incline sharpened as the road approached the base of a wide mountain. Black dots pitted the looming rockface, remains of the original 19th century mineral claims that had been abandoned after they sunk the main shaft on the opposite side of the peak. She'd never liked those holes, even before the history lessons Grace had given them illuminating the mine's nefarious origins. The idea of sleeping so close to them made her skin crawl. But she wasn't in any position to complain.

The truck turned onto a quiet cul-de-sac, then eased into the third driveway on the left in front of a two-story townhouse.

"Here we are," Cooper said, killing the engine. "It's not much, but we'll do our best to make you feel at home until we can find you a more permanent situation."

Cari nodded. The house was old and narrow, with barely a foot of dirt separating it from its neighbors. Still, the front porch didn't sag, and the mocha paint job looked relatively fresh. Compared to the rest of the houses on the block, it was one of the nicest.

"It's lovely," she said.

"Thanks." He unbuckled his seatbelt, then paused. "There is one more thing. My wife doesn't know about what we do, or what specifically killed your mom. So, while you live here, you *will* have to do...you know, normal kid stuff, once you're ready. School, and homework…and cut back on work hours for a while. Okay?"

She sucked in her breath. The thought of going back to school excited her. The thought of homework excited her much less. And the thought of taking a hiatus from Edensgate…

"I get it," she said softly. "Not sure I like it, but you're right. It's probably for the best."

Cooper nodded stiffly. He grabbed the box at her feet and exited the cab.

She followed him up the creaky porch steps to the front door. As she entered the dimly lit foyer, a dark-haired woman in sweats and a red thermal top swooped out of the kitchen doorway with her arms out.

"Hi! You must be Cari."

Cari skidded to a halt with a started cry, her hands shooting up to block the advance.

"Ally," Cooper whispered, a gentle warning in his tone.

The woman stopped. A look of horrified embarrassment turned her face as red as her shirt, and she yanked her arms back. "Oh my God, I'm so sorry. I didn't mean to scare you. I was just, um…"

Hug. Cari dropped her hands. *She was going to hug me.*

"Anyway," Ally said, trying to reclaim her composure. "Cooper told me about the…accident, at your house. If there's anything you need, anything at all…"

She let the sentence fade beneath a half-smile that shone like a beacon of warmth and kindness. Cari wanted to accept it and respond in kind, but she couldn't quite manage through the icy numbness that surrounded her. All she could offer was a stiff "Thanks."

"You're welcome." Ally gestured to the staircase. "The guest room is all ready for you. I'm sure you must be exhausted. Up the stairs, take a right, and it's the first door across the hall. Or—would you like me to show you?"

"That's okay," Cari said, taking the box from Cooper. "I'll find it."

She took the steps two at a time. No offense to Ally, but she'd had enough human interaction for one day in general—and, it seemed, way too much with one person in particular.

Ascending from the warmth and light of the first floor to the cool, peaceful dimness of the second felt like walking into a dream. Unlike the bouncy, carpeted metal floor of the trailer, the wood planks of the second story landing felt solid and steady beneath Cari's feet.

The door to the guest room—her room—stood slightly ajar. She used the corner of the box to nudge it the rest of the way. The scent of vanilla and lilac enveloped her immediately. Across from her, a full wall of windows overlooked a small rear garden. To her right was a walk-in closet; to the left, a wrought-iron bed that was easily the size of her entire old room. Nudging the door shut, she set her box on top of a tall chest of drawers and sat down on the puffy white duvet. It practically swallowed her.

She'd never seen a more beautiful bedroom. It was so cozy, so welcoming. So…

Not her.

She curled her fingers into the duvet as her breath turned to shallow gasps and black splotches bloomed in front of her. With all the strength she could summon, she burst upward, ripping the blanket off the bed as she did so. Grabbing her box of stuff, she dashed into the walk-in closet and slammed the door behind her.

"Thank you for agreeing to this," Cooper murmured toward Ally as Cari disappeared upstairs. "I promise, it'll only be a couple of weeks. Just until—"

"Don't worry about it."

He frowned. He had been prepared to defend his position, citing Grace's miniscule one-room hut and the fact that John's house had suffered so much neglect over the years that the last dusting of snow had almost caused the roof to cave in. But when he'd called to tell Ally about the situation, she'd agreed to help without hesitation. In fact, he'd barely even gotten the question out before she jumped on it. And now she wasn't concerned about the time frame? Something was up.

He turned to look at his wife. Her smile had collapsed, the welcoming warmth she'd shown Cari now buried under stony suspicion. Cooper shuddered as the temperature in the room dropped twenty degrees.

"An hour at most, Cooper," she said, her voice low. "That's what you told me. That's what you *promised*."

He sucked in his breath, giving himself a moment before answering. "Something came up at work. They needed me."

Her face constricted, not in a scowl or a pout, but in defeat. "They? Or *she*?"

The word backhanded him across the face. Anger seared through him as he took a calculated step toward her. "Cari's not the only person that lost someone today, you know. Lola asked me to help, so I helped."

She spat out a bitter chuckle. "It's not *Lola* I'm talking about, and you damn well know it."

His jaw dropped as indignant heat crept over his face and neck. He took deep breaths, trying desperately to diffuse the feeling. A barrage of thoughts cascaded through his mind that, though numerous, mostly fell along one of two lines.

"What is that supposed to mean?" was the one he chose to vocalize.

Ally wrapped her arms around her chest and mounted the stairs. "Forget it. I've got to get ready for work. Just...*call* next time, okay?"

She disappeared into the dark, ending the conversation, at least for the moment. He looked up after her as his second line of thinking, the one he couldn't say, would *never* say, continued to run.

How the hell did she know?

Chapter Thirteen

Grace tossed her bag on the dilapidated futon that took up most of her living room and headed for the kitchenette. Her stomach growled as she grabbed a jar of peanut butter, shoveled two fingers-worth into her mouth, and stared absently out her kitchen window at the neighboring backyard. That house had been abandoned for years, as had most of the houses on the block, and the small patch of grass was completely overrun with weeds. When she'd first moved in, she had imagined that someday she would annex the dwelling as storage space for all the stuff that didn't fit in her own tiny house. Eight years later, and that day had not yet come to pass. Turns out she didn't need nearly as much as she once thought she did.

Brrrring!

She stiffened as the jangle of her kitchen phone shattered the morning stillness.

"Nuh aguhn," she groaned around the sticky sweet paste coating on her tongue. She wished she could let it ring itself to death. But if something had gone wrong with Cari (or Nelson, or any one of a dozen other things), she'd rather know about it.

"What's wrong?" she answered, licking the last of the peanut butter from her index finger.

"Why don't you tell me?"

The deep, sultry voice on the other end of the line made her insides quake.

"Lola." She wiped her hand on the front of her coveralls. "Uh, hi. How…how are you?"

"Oh, I'm super," Lola shot back. *"I love riding ten hours through the desert in a para-shuttle. It's a dream come true."*

"Uh, yeah." Grace bit the inside of her cheek as memories gathered in the back of her mind, looming like pregnant storm clouds. "Cooper told me you called. Sorry I didn't have the chance to call you back yet. I was working, and, well…"

"Yeah, I know. Believe me, I don't want to be talking to you either. But…" She sighed heavily. *"Look, I'm not going to pretend to know much about that fucked up town, or what kind of weird shit my dad was involved with. But I know enough that when some random wild thought stabs me in the brain over and over again, I'm gonna do whatever it tells me. So here goes. And I'm only going to say this once, so write it down."*

"Okay. Hang on a sec." Grace rifled through the dirty dishes sprawled across the counter until she found a Sharpie and a takeout menu from a long-defunct Indian restaurant. "Go ahead."

"First National Bank of Halcyon. Employee Picnic. 2008." She spat the words into the phone like they were poison. *"There, responsibility over. And Grace?"*

"Yeah?"

"Do not come to the funeral."

The line went dead.

Grace stared down at the receiver in her shaking hand. The mental thunderhead split open, unleashing a torrent of images. Torn flesh. Broken bones. Lola crying. And her hammer.

In her own hand.

"It wasn't my idea," she whispered to no one. "It wasn't..."

She pitched into the counter, her chest tight and her breathing thin. The visions pulsed, stronger and stronger, as if trying to pull her back, body and soul, into one of the most horrible moments of her life. Her panicked eyes dragged the room for anything to keep her in the present. They landed on the counter and found Lola's words scrawled in black across the menu.

First National Bank of Halcyon. Employee Picnic. 2008.

She repeated them in her head, over and over like a mantra, until the panic receded and her mind settled itself back into a normal rhythm. *First National Bank.* That's where Nelson had worked. *Employee Picnic. 2008*

What the hell did *that* mean?

She tested her legs and found herself stable enough to walk. Grabbing the menu and the peanut butter jar, she sat down at the small table nestled between the kitchenette and the living room and typed the words into her cell phone browser. "First National Bank of Halcyon" came up with a number of hits, but none of them included the word "picnic." She scrolled through the results with one hand while dipping peanut butter out of the jar with the other. Not exactly a well-balanced breakfast, but after that little death march down memory lane, it made her feel a lot better. She slogged through three pages of search results, clicking on the links that seemed most promising—and coming up empty. She slammed her phone on the table. How did Simon do it day after day after day? At least he had the advantage of knowing what he was looking for. This would take forever, with what little she had to go on.

What little Lola had given her.

She sighed and rubbed her eyes. Even if she could set aside everything that had transpired between them, Lola had just lost her father. If her one request was that Grace spending a day googling some weird phrase, how could she say no?

She retrieved the phone—and the hairs on the back of her neck prickled. When she slammed it on the table, she must have accidentally hit the Image Results button. A young Libby Hembert filled the screen, toasting the camera with a bottle of Perrier.

"Son of a bitch," Grace whispered, cradling the phone as if it had turned to pure gold. She couldn't believe how healthy Libby looked, grinning at the camera, her cheeks flushed and teeth brilliant white. Her free arm hung across the shoulders of a bearded strawberry blond man, presumably her husband. He held her by the waist with one hand while pumping a spatula in the air like a trophy with the other. They wore matching white baseball caps and red T-shirts with "Getting Things Cooking at the FNB 2008 Friends and Family Picnic" printed across the chest.

So what?

Grace returned their smiles with a scowl. So, Libby worked at the bank too. Big deal. Sure, it was kind of a surreal picture under the circumstances, but what did that have to do with—

Her eyes snagged on something over Libby's right shoulder that stopped her cold. She reverse-pinched the screen, zooming in to make sure she had seen it right.

She had. Nelson's hair was thicker and his gut significantly less pronounced, but it was definitely him. He wore the same red shirt as the couple—and so did the little girl standing in front of him. A tiny thing with blond pigtails and giant blue eyes, Cari was practically drowning in the red fabric as she reached up with both hands to accept the popsicle Nelson offered to her.

She must not have seen the thing hovering just behind him.

The image trembled as Grace's hand started to shake. Perhaps it had only appeared after the fact, isolated by the click of the camera. Or maybe Cari had mistaken it for a shadow. Which Grace might have done as well, if not for the egg-white eyes and ragged smile. Heart pounding, she traced its feathery limbs down Nelson's arms to where they sunk like tattoos into his hands.

And Cari's.

Grace collapsed backward with such force it sent her chair rocking on its rear legs. She gulped at the air, trying to stave off panic, as her own words blared in her ears like a siren.

Anyone could be infected.
And we'd never know.

***

Thanks for reading The Mourning Sun!

Want to see what the gang is up to next?
Turn the page to read a sample from
Part V: A Midwinter Nightmare

Or scan the code below to buy the book now.

The soft patter of feet roused Cari from groggy non-sleep. They stopped for a moment, then continued down the hall. Allie did this every night on her way to bed, pausing outside Cari's room as if she wanted to peek in and say goodnight, but couldn't quite bring herself to do it. Probably for the best. Were she to work up the courage to open the door, she'd just find a stripped mattress and an empty room. It wasn't that Cari didn't appreciate the generosity of a big bedroom of her own. She did. But after sleeping in a retrofitted storage unit for eight years, she felt much more at home in a smaller space.

Cari yawned and stretched, pressing her stocking feet against the closed closet door as she listened to the rest of Allie's bedtime routine: running water, the stifled hum of an electric toothbrush, a flushing toilet, the static murmur of the evening news. In about fifteen minutes the murmur would stop, and everything would be silent.

She craned her head toward the low shelf where a normal person would keep their shoes, but where she kept her alarm clock. 8:30. Right on time. If only she could sleep like that.

Or at all.

Her head felt like a detached balloon as she searched the knot of quilt and pillows, trying to find where she'd dropped her latest trashy novel. She couldn't sleep, but the books helped put her into a kind of browned-out stupor that at least stopped her mind from bothering her for a few hours. Her weary eyes caught on the bare bulb hanging from the ceiling.

"Dammit!" she cried, screwing the palms of her hands into her sockets to dull the pain throbbing through her exhausted retinas.

"Cari…"

That was the same voice she'd heard yesterday in the living room. Gravelly, distorted, but also sort of…familiar.

"Cari." The word accompanied a long, loud creak of a floorboard—directly on the other side of the closet door.

Heart pounding, she lowered her hands from her eyes. A shuffle of shadows interrupted the light filtering in under the closet door.

It's in my room.

Her eyes trailed upward. The doorknob squeaked and jerked violently to the right.

"Shit!" She flung herself forward, grabbing the knob with both hands and twisting it in the other direction.

A wordless screech of frustration ripped through the stillness as a furious weight slammed against the door. Her socks snagged on the splintered floorboards as she braced herself against the invading force.

Please, Allie, she begged as the smooth metal rubbed her palms raw. *Please tell me you can hear this.*

Another slam made the hinges groan. She couldn't hold on anymore. One more hit and it would be in. Whimpering, she braced herself for the assault.

Then everything went silent.

She pressed her ear to the wood, straining to hear into the room over her own heavy breathing. Was it over? Had it left? Or was it simply pretending, lulling her into a false sense of security while it lay in wait on the other side?

Cold air blasted her toes. She looked down. The shadow was gone, replaced by a wash of pale light that didn't match the warmth of the bedside lamp.

She took a steadying breath. False security or not, she couldn't stay in the closet forever. She had to look.

Grasping the knob with her sore palms, she leaned back and ripped the door open.

The parted curtains rippled as a winter breeze swept through the empty room.

But the curtains are always closed. And I definitely wouldn't have the window open on such a cold night.

She tiptoed across the room and peered out. The glow of the near-full moon illuminated the small garden below. Really, it was just a small patch of concrete and some grapevines that grew up the two-story trellises leaning against the house. Near the gate that led to the back alley hunched a dark figure as black as a shadow, even in the light of the full moon. Its shapeless clothes and hood disguised its face along with all other identifying features. At this distance, she couldn't even tell if it was a man or a woman.

"Cari."

She exhaled in a whoosh as tears sprung to her eyes.

It *was* a voice she recognized.

"Mom?"

The shadow slipped over the gate like oil and disappeared down the alley.

Her heart throbbed in her chest. Before she could think to stop herself, her stocking feet found their footing on the trellis and carried her down.

"This is so stupid," she muttered as she dropped onto the cold stone patio. But that wasn't quite accurate. Chasing down an ethereal being alone, with no shoes, no coat, and no backup was so far beyond stupid, they hadn't come up with a word for it. But that thing had the voice of her mother.

Why?

She flipped up the lock on the gate and jogged off down the alley, wincing as the loose gravel dug into her soles. Stupid or not, she had to know the answer.

Scan here to buy Part V: A Midwinter Nightmare

Acknowledgments

Thanks to Taisha, Mike, Wolf, Kevin, Richard, Xander, and the whole of the Sin City Writers Group for their insightful critiques and friendly but firm reminders of "you can do better than that."

To Jami at Chimera Editing for her spot-on suggestions and gentle nudges in the right direction. How you know where I need to go before I do, I'll never figure out.

To Joseph, who took my half-baked idea for a redesign and turned it into moving, gorgeous art.

And finally, to Marcin. You are a good person and people say nice things about you.

The Mourning Sun was in large part produced during the winter and spring of 2020, a period that I imagine will one day be known as the Covid Pandemic of 2020. In this time of struggle and stress, it would have been so easy to bury myself in the couch and hibernate until it was all over. Luckily, I found myself riding through the plague surrounded by passionate writers and artists who were determined to continue doing amazing things regardless of what the world threw at us. It was that energy that kept me going when things got bad, and it is what I want most to acknowledge and celebrate now.

The story has gotten darker, but it doesn't end here.
The only way out is through.

S.G. Tasz
June 16th, 2020

About the Author

S.G. Tasz is a graduate of Lawrence University in Appleton, Wisconsin. Previous writing credits include the web series *Chic*, the award-winning 48-hour Film Project "A Fairly Normal Love Story," and several pieces of short fiction. In addition to plotting the *Dead Mawl* gang's next adventure, she is also working on her debut novel, an excerpt for which was the top selection for the 2019 Writer's Bloc Anthology. She lives in Las Vegas with her husband, two cats, and a turtle.

About the Illustrator

Joseph Reedy is an artist based out of Madison, Wisconsin primarily working in the video game and music industries. He also pets lots of doggos.

***

For the latest news, subscribe to my email newsletter at **www.sgtasz.com.**

Made in the USA
Middletown, DE
14 November 2024